THREE STORIES

BY EDWARD GILCHRIST WRIGHT

RoseDog Books
PITTSBURGH, PENNSYLVANIA 15238

RoseDog Books
585 Alpha Drive
Suite 103
Pittsburgh, PA 15238
Visit our website at *www.rosedogbookstore.com*

ISBN: 979-8-89027-041-2
eISBN: 979-8-89027-539-4

THREE STORIES

TABLE OF CONTENTS

Devotion

— ⁓ —

THE POPULATION OF PAGE (3,621) WAS SURPRISED WHEN Reverend Phil, a widower for nearly six years, married a woman half his age.

Philip Fairfield, a graduate of Faith Seminary, had been the head of red-brick Page Methodist Church since 1948, upon the demise of the beloved Reverend Balcolm. Reverend Fairfield, or Reverend Phil as he was affectionately known to parishioners, had come to Page accompanied by his wife April Mae and their six-year old son Dickie. Unfortunately, the former April Mae Bunny died in the spring of 1952, leaving Reverend Phil to raise a ten-year old boy and supervise a 90-year old institution alone. The cause of April Mae's untimely death was uncertain, though there were medical assumptions, everything from bad heart to exhaustion. The town was undecided. As it turned out, Reverend Phil didn't exactly retire to a monastery after April Mae's death. Instead he had a long relationship with widow Shirley Lee Shawnsee, a relationship only vaguely comprehended in Page, a town of limited comprehension.

Mrs Shawnsee was a faithful member of the Page Methodist congregation and supported Reverend Phil in his many projects. She was an amateur artist and had completed a day-glo reproduction of the Last Supper, which Reverend Phil pronounced "Wonderful! Beautiful!". The Page Methodist Church had no refectory so Shirley Lee's masterpiece was placed over the inside entrance of the church, just under a small rose window, where it could be admired by the parishioners when they congregated as well as by the choir when it essayed hymns from behind the altar. This group, the faded, the atonal could gaze at the false daVinci while they sang:

"And he walks with me and he talks with me

and he tells me I am his own;

And the joy we share as we tarry there

None other has ever known!"

Now, don't even suggest it! The love here is ethereal love, and the suitor is the Son of God himself. And don't question why this deity would be prowling around a garden "while the dew is still on the roses". He seemed to have an affinity for gardens. The choir never questioned the lyrics, and certainly Reverend Phil never did. They may seem transparent to some, but to Reverend Phil's parishioners, over-fed and under-read, the lyrics meant one obvious thing: they were loved.

Hands clasped behind his back, head cocked, beaming, blinking, that was Reverend Phil. But behind the rustic façade rested a fierce Republican nature. When a celebrated actress betrayed her husband (with an <u>Italian</u>!) Reverend Phil denounced her from the pulpit as a shameless hussy, warning his flock not to support her latest ballyhooed Hollywood production, an epic in which she played a saint — a saint, no less!

He also thought electrocution was too good for the Rosenbergs. They should be dragged into a public square and slowly stoned to death. His flock bent its collective head and nodded, like sheep awaiting the ax. Needless to say, the Reverend worshipped the administration, both the President and his Vice President. "Good, honest guys," Reverend Phil decided.

Standing a block and a half from the Church grounds was the

manse, built in 1910 for the comfort of Reverend Balcolm, inherited by Reverend Phil when he took over his clerical duties, a two-story wooden structure painted white and consisting (on the ground floor) of a living room, a dining room, an adjacent kitchen, and a puce-hued study where Reverend Phil composed his sermons on an ancient Remington. Upstairs included four bedrooms, and in the basement there was a furnished apartment. There were three "comfort stations", one on each level. A screened-in porch enclosed half the house, one door of which served as entrance from the kitchen to the small garage. Reverend Phil owned a 1950 Ford.

It was the assumption of Shirley Lee Shawnsee that she should be moving into the manse as Reverend Phil's second wife, but alas! this was not to be. In the spring Reverend Phil had attended a Don't Drink Rally in the capital and there he had met dark-haired Elizabeth Dawson and her dark-haired brother Anthony. Betty and Tony had been orphaned (at 25 years and 23 years respectively) when their parents died two weeks apart, one from emphysema, the other from heartbreak. They both lived in the capital, Betty in an apartment house near Hamilton Square, Tony in a dorm on the campus of State, where he was a student working under a state scholarship. Betty held down a job in a fashionable ladies' store on the main street, the Élégance. Reverend Phil was quite impressed by the youth and sincerity of the two assumed prohibitionists and invited them to dinner at the manse one Friday evening (Mandy serving her classic and greasy fried chicken), then to a service at the Page Methodist Church one Sunday morning (Topic: "Why Alcohol is Bad for our Boys and Girls"). From there it was just a matter of days before Betty (only) was escorted to a Sunday School picnic and later to a Bible study meeting. It soon became evident that Reverend Phil had evolved into a suitor, and Betty could see that he had not only an awed reputation but a very comfortable home. She became acquiescent. Except for Shirley Lee, the Methodist matrons and maidens of Page began hovering around Betty, seeing her as the future power behind the pulpit. And sure enough in the lovely month of June Betty became the second Mrs Fairfield, Reverend Phil's friend Mr Jones, a Justice of the Peace, performing the ceremony, which was held in Reverend Phil's church, the chapel bursting with rosebuds, the organ cranking out Mendelssohn, a supervisor from Élégance serving as matron of honor, lanky flop-haired Tony as best man, shifting from foot to foot.

Standing aside, completely uninvolved, could be seen a somewhat thin pale boy beneath a stained glass representation of a fable from Luke depicting an elderly man dressed in scarlet and gold embracing a half-naked youth. The boy observer himself was wearing a dark suit and a white shirt buttoned at the collar. The idea of crisp jeans or a short-sleeved plaid shirt was out of the question. After all, this was Reverend Phil's son Dickie, hair carefully clipped, living in moral superiority to all other sixteen-year olds. It should be explained that "Dickie" was not a sobriquet, it was the son's birth name. The former April Mae Bunny had wanted to give her boy a cute friendly name so that people would like him. Well, Dickie had the name but no one particularly liked him. With his chilly stare and cold ripostes Dickie was not exactly what the citizens of Page considered a proper pastor's son. Now he stood and watched his father marry a twenty-six year old girl who was probably a fool and had no idea what she was headed into. Dickie knew.

"Hey, Dickie," Reverend Phil called out, signaling to his son, "come on over here and kiss your new mama." Dickie strode over, gave Betty the kiss of ice, and disappeared into the congregation, not even glancing at his father or his new brother-in-law.

Perhaps the Reverend thought it would be in bad taste to hold the reception at the manse. At any rate, it was held at Roy's on the outskirts of town, the guests driving there and parking in the adjacent lot, beneath the big kidney-shaped sign. Mandy, of course, could not be a guest, but she and two of her friends were compensated by helping Roy's employees arrange the "boo-fay" and set up the lemonade and root beer counters. On the lawn outside were placed tables and straight-back chairs and here the guests hunched forward, gossiped, and spilled food.

Betty the Bride and her Beloved retired to the manse to begin their lives together. After all, Betty had to learn her new responsibilities, and she did. First of all, she learned that Mandy may be the cook but that the new bride was the dietary chef and therefore decided what was bought at market and placed on the table. Two of Mandy's relatives came in once a week to clean the manse (twenty-five dollars a week, to split between them) but Betty had to supervise the washing, dusting, and polishing and if anything was lacking the girls were told. Also, Betty took dictation from Reverend Phil, sorted his mail, typed up his notes and made sure the sermon was ready for Sunday morning. If everything wasn't ready Betty was told. As for her position at Élégance that was gone. No wife of Reverend Phil's was going to work, not in the proletarian sense. Mrs Phil had enough to keep her busy.

Betty bided her time, waiting until two months after the wedding to take her wifely prerogative: she suggested to Reverend Phil that it would be a good idea if Tony moved from the dorm on State campus and lived in the basement apartment, an arrangement the siblings had been discussing for a month. For bed and board Tony could offer $100.00 a month, and it would be really convenient for everyone.

Reverend Phil pulled off his spectacles, stared at her for a few moments, then said: "But, Sweetheart, the basement apartment is for Gritz."

Gritz? Who was Gritz?

Gritz was George Fairfield, the Reverend's elder brother, elder by seven years. Gritz lived in a boarding house in the capital, but it was becoming increasingly difficult for him to move around and also to pay his meager rent. He had had to relinquish his custodian job at a local wholesale drug company in April and his bank account was ebbing. Gritz had not been invited to and therefore had not attended his brother's wedding, and Betty had never heard of him till now.

But there he was. Gritz moved into the manse a week before Labor Day, settling into the basement apartment, which he immediately found uncomfortable. Craggy, gray-haired, turning to fat, Gritz complained about the bed, the food, the stairs, the bathroom.

"Don't worry about a thing, Gritz," Reverend Phil assured him. "That's what Betty's here for. Right, Sweetheart?"

"Right!" Betty answered as rage rose within her. It had become obvious: that was what she was here for. She wanted her brother for company and for moral support, and all she had now was cranky Gritz, who complained to her, and ice-cold Dickie, who barely spoke to her.

Of the two other bedrooms on the top floor one was "spare" and the other was used for storage, so Tony stayed in the dorm with his textbooks and his "roomie" a loquacious youth from New York.

The day after Labor Day Dickie returned to Page High School for his junior year. Page High was located at the head of Wilkin Street, a squat red-brick porticoed building cluttered with official looking windows; one of these windows facing out onto the portico itself, indicated the office of Principal Peter Cowper, "Skip" to his friends. Principal Cowper's primary concern at Page was to make certain his two student-sons always received preferential treatment in everything. The two boys Leonard and Benjamin — Len and Ben — never had to worry about being reprimanded or burdened with undue responsibility. Principal Skip saw to that.

Among the traditions at Page High was for each student to be assigned a counselor in the first week and to set a meeting with that sage in order to determine his or her future at the school as well as in the great vista of life. Miss Ann Farro had been chosen for Dickie and he was to meet her in her classroom at four on a Tuesday afternoon.

Miss Farro, thin and thirty years old, had all the suppressed imagination of an actress out of work. She had been an impressionable child when she saw a sentimental screen drama set during the 19th Century in which the star portrayed a teacher in an American girls' school aware that all the students were gossiping about a scandal in the teacher's past. The *professeur* gathered all the girls together in the classroom, sat behind her desk, and went into flashback: as a governess in a French duke's opulent home she had earned not only the love of her charges but of the paterfamilias himself and consequently the fury of the duchess. This culminated in murder or suicide or both, Miss Farro couldn't exactly remember, but the flashback ending, all the students crowded around their teacher, weeping and begging forgiveness. Little Ann was spellbound.

Then, as a twenty-eight year old, it happened Miss Farro and biology teacher Bob Duster worked together on an environmental project, supervising committees, creating posters, etc. Now, Mr Duster was a bit of biology himself, separated from his wife, and that's all it took: when the two of them were seen huddled in the cafeteria, the girls began gossiping ruthlessly. A man separated from his wife, the perfect chance for a potential homebreaker.

It didn't take long for the gossip to get back to Miss Farro. Cooly, she entered her full classroom, seated herself behind her desk, and went into flashback: when she was an eighteen-year old girl Miss Farro had developed a relationship with a wild boy who rode a motorcycle and smoked cigarettes. Ann's parents, of course, disapproved but Ann was in love. She and the boy had come close to eloping when one Saturday afternoon the boy had been killed in a crash. All this was related with dramatic rests and glances at the ceiling. When she had finished she folded her hands, closed her eyes, and whispered: "Class dismissed". The students did <u>not</u> gather around her weeping and imploring forgiveness. They simply filed out and gossiped some more. As for Miss Farro, she was elated. At long last she was the tragic heroine, revealing her long lost love.

But that wasn't the end. Miss Farro went through the same recitation class after class. Another teacher was not amused and complained to Mr Cowper. "But, Sir, she's not teaching, she's conducting a soap opera."

"Aw, she's a good girl," Skip replied. "Let her have her – aw, let her be!" (Mr Duster, by the way, returned to his wife and his home town and was never thought of again, least of all by Miss Farro.)

The teacher was seated at her desk when Dickie kept their appointment. Dickie sat stiffly in a child's combination chair and desk which was set beside Miss Farro's more authoritarian throne. "Well, Dickie, welcome to another year at good ole Page. Have you thought about school a lot over the summer?"

"No."

A light laugh. "Oh, I bet not! But it's exciting to be back, isn't it? All the fun we'll have?"

No answer.

"So. So, Dickie, your future. Well, I suppose you want to be a good pastor like your dad."

"No."

"Oh. You don't want to teach the ways of our Lord to his flock?"

"No."

"Oh. Well, what do you suppose you'd like to do?"

"I don't … know."

"Oh. Well, let's start with school. Would you like to be a Confederate?"

"No. I don't like football."

"Oh. Well, maybe you'd like to join Mrs Sherman's Dramatics class?"

"No. I don't like dramatics."

"Oh. Well, maybe you'd like to join our Spanish Club?"

"No. I don't like Spanish."

"Oh. Well, maybe you could join the band."

"I like drums."

"Oh? Well, maybe you could join the band."

"I like them fast. Fast and loud."

"Well, of course you'd play them the way Mr Nelson trained you."

"I don't … know."

At this point Miss Farro hesitated. "Well, Dickie …"

"Is that all?"

"Well, yes, for the time being, that's all. Oh, and Dickie, you'll see. We're going to have a great school year."

The interview was over, the wisdom dispensed.

Dickie shoved back the desk and walked away.

Over his shoulder: "Thanks."

Sadly, the year did not progress as well as Miss Farro had predicted. In fact, a disaster occurred.

Nearing the end of September the cafeteria was becoming crowded one noontide, teachers and pupils queuing up to pay their dollar for either burnt macaroni or scalded chicken. At one table were Ellen McSward and Arnold Miller engulfed in each other's fascination. Lottie Haymaker, garishly rouged and dressed in red polka dots and layered crinolines, swooped uninvited onto the cheerleaders' table with a grinning "Howdy!" Lottie was <u>not</u> a cheerleader, but she wanted to associate with the popular girls, perhaps to decrease her image. "Oh, my!" Joyce Simons sighed, eyes rolling slightly. The other girls just smiled.

Members of the Confederates or Cons were seated at a nearby table, all shoulders and crew cuts, and one of them winked at Joyce sympathetically. They all sneered at Lottie, comparing her with the beauty having lunch with their quarterback friend Arnold.

There was a special oblong table near the cafeteria's entrance that was called the Teachers' Table. Here Miss Farro, Mrs Sherman and the librarian Miss Goetz sat together, discreetly dining and discussing school matters.

The hicks from an outlying area and who were naturally ostracized by the Page elite, were in a far corner, in their overalls, shirts made of chicken feed sacks and soup-bowl haircuts. A special bus brought them from the farmyards onto the school entrance every morning to be looked down at and avoided.

Everything was loud, scornful and superficially friendly when suddenly the air was pierced by a terrified scream. It came from the kitchen, and a few moments later a big black man, Clyde by name, wearing a wide greasy apron, stumbled from the kitchen also, yelling "Getit! Getit!" People rose from their seats and stared. Lottie was the first diner to yell, and yell she could, scrambling as well as possible with crinolines, onto her chair. Then the others saw it and pandemonium set in.

A large gray rat had scurried around the cashier's desk and was racing, zig-zagging across the cafeteria floor, through tables and chairs as both teachers and students screamed and scrambled out of the way, climbing onto furniture, holding onto each other and attempting not to fall over. The Cons were as desperate as the cheerleaders to avoid contact with the rodent and the air was filled with the four-letter familiarities of adolescence.

Pausing in terror, its glittering eyes darting back and forth, the rat rose for a moment in defiance, flaunting its paws and wiggling its nose. Then it was off again, heading from one group of diners to the other, causing frantic shifts of movement. The phone on the wall began ringing. People were calling out: "Do Something! DO something!"

"What th' hell ya want me to do?" bellowed a Con as he climbed onto a table.

Finally against a wall the rat had trapped himself into a corner, and one of the hicks calmly picked up a chair. Judging space and weight, the farmer's blond boy lifted his weapon and threw it violently forward. Bull's eye! It was a mess, of course, but the kitchen's colored staff cleaned it up and the problem was solved. Almost.

When the news got out about a rat running loose in the cafeteria — and emerging from the kitchen – Principal Cowper's office was jammed with phone calls from the Department of Public Health, the School Board and the capital's <u>Today</u>. He was personally castigated. And if that wasn't enough hand-made posters appeared in the school's corridors: How Clean is the Kitchen? No Mice in the Rice! Hey, Rat, no Rats!

Dickie had not been present during the fiasco. He usually took a sandwich and oreos to an empty classroom and had his lunch there. Because Dickie was the Reverend Phil's son girls did not attempt to flirt with him and boys didn't tell him the latest joke, the one about the plumber and the pussy cat.

So Dickie lunched alone and read. And what did Dickie read? Well, he had stopped going to his father's services at the age of thirteen and had no interest in the Saturday Morning Bible Studies. Dickie's reading had taken another turn. He had heard of a certain British philosopher and was curious to enter his works. But when he questioned Miss Goetz about the philosopher she gave Dickie a very odd look and said "Well, Dickie, our library doesn't include such authors, never will. I'm surprised the Reverend would ... oh, well."

His next move was to question his brother-in-law, his step-brother, whatever Tony was. One evening Betty's brother had been invited to dinner and afterwards, in the privacy of the screened-in porch Dickie had asked Tony about any bookstores in the capital where he might find the works he was seeking. Tony gave him a sly but friendly smile. "Oh, you mean the GeeGee."

And that's how Dickie became acquainted with the Grateful Ghost on the State campus, a cluttered dusty book-crammed shop near Tony's dorm. With part of his allowance Dickie purchased Why I Am Not A Christian. He hid it from the students at school, and at the manse he stored it under the bed, as a Con might keep pornography.

Dickie was seated in a corner of an empty schoolroom one noon when the door suddenly opened and there stood a balding spreading man, mid-forties, who looked in and said: "Whatcha doin' here?"

Dickie gave him a cold stare: "Reading."

Coach Templar stared some more, then added: "Huh?"

No response.

"Oh, hey, you're that Methodist preacher's son, ain't ya? Reading, huh? Well, yeah, it's a good book. Yeah, a good book. I'll bet your dad's proud of you."

No response.

"Uh … you ain't a Con, are ya? Ah, no, I guess you're not. No, no definitely not." With a low chuckle, Coach Templar slowly closed the door.

No, had Dickie been a Confederate he would have been well acquainted with Coach Templar as were all the heroes. The teacher was nicknamed Coach Kickoff due to his favorite means of discipline – i.e., giving someone a good kick in the pants. Even quarterback Arnold Miller, acknowledged as the best player on the team, did not escape this mode of discipline. (But even though Arnold was acknowledged the best, the team captain of course was the principal's clumsy son Leonard Cowper, and Coach Templar did not <u>dare</u> try to discipline him. He would have lost his job immediately.) There were rumors that Coach's correction methods even extended to his domestic circle, for instance if Mrs Templar brought home sausage instead of franks. Coach's wife explained frequent injuries with tales of slipping on the stairs for bruises and standing too close to the stove for burns. As for Coach Kickoff's professional prowess, last season his team had played ten games and won two. Was it that important? Certainly. High-school football was to Page what the Olympics are to the world.

Football was the cause of changes in the manse. Whereas Reverend Phil had no interest in the gridiron brother Gritz was fascinated and insisted on a "sight-sound thing" being installed in his basement apartment so that he could watch professional games. The black-and-white reception was inadequate and the sound uncertain, but Gritz would sit in his armchair and bellow at the players, who inevitably did not follow his instructions. Sometimes Tony would join him but would have to sit on the edge of the bed and would have to help old Gritz to the toilet, duties which discouraged him from enjoying the sport.

There was another problem: Gritz wanted to drink beer, a great deal of beer, while he cheered or chastised the Green Bay Packers, and Reverend Phil had mandated No Alcohol! in the holy manse. Gritz became increasingly truculent, creating all kinds of scenes. So that finally Betty – who was responsible for keeping the apartment clean and freshly supplied – told her husband she couldn't stand it anymore: Gritz had to be allowed his beer. The Reverend had reluctantly agreed on the stipulation that it would not be tolerated upstairs. Fine. Betty would bring down the meals <u>with</u> beer two times a day (Gritz rose too late to even consider breakfast), help Gritz to the toilet, clean the toilet, then give the apartment a quick cleaning before she returned upstairs to supervise Mandy, make sure the Reverend's meals were served, take dictation, and type up sermons and church bulletins. When she had time she would make small repairs around the manse and go out and do the shopping. Twice a week the Ladies Bible Club would meet to discuss how to challenge social problems in Page and how best to censor books and newspapers. Betty was expected to supervise these meetings.

Thanksgiving was another story altogether. A huge feast was held in the church yard itself, sponsored by donations, and Betty had to supervise the purchasing, preparation and deployment of the turkey, potatoes, dressing, cranberries, townhouse rolls, and cider. She, of course, with other Page ladies served the food, while the men sat at oblong tables and talked.

It was about this time that Betty, as she took Gritz his refreshments, would hold aside a beer for herself. The only person she confessed this to was Tony, who gave her his sly smile and said "Prosit!" (Though he was having a little difficulty with Agricultural Ecology he was moving right along with his foreign toasts.)

First it was a single beer for Betty, then a couple. Gritz, who never ventured upstairs anymore, soon began to complain that his supply of beer was going awfully fast. "Ya drinkin' my beer?" he bluntly asked Betty.

"Just a couple," Betty answered in a placating tone. "Hey, don't tell him, huh?"

Gritz started snuffling, oddly giggling. "Don't worry, girl! Drink all ya want. It'll be our secret."

After that she had Tony bring a card table down from the storage room to the basement apartment and she would sit there drinking beer and watching football, which she didn't understand. Reverend Phil was kept in the dark.

One afternoon after Thanksgiving Betty asked permission to go to the capital with the car: a lady she knew was having a holiday party and Betty had been invited. There was no party. Once Betty parked the Ford near Hamilton Square she walked to a nearby hardware store where she had the car keys duplicated. She would never ask permission to take the car out again. From the hardware store she strolled slowly over to Howie's, a bar across the street from the square, where she drank beer for an hour. She didn't mean for it to happen, but she struck up a conversation with a trucker who was passing through town. He invited her to a motel where he was staying, and she accepted. Later he gave her enough money to take a taxi back to the square; she slept in the Ford for an hour, then returned to the manse.

Another afternoon she didn't go to Howie's but just sat in the square on a bench. A paunchy middle-aged man wearing eyeglasses strolled by, glanced at her, strolled back and sat down beside her. How was she? She was okay. Was she waiting for someone? No. The man was spending the afternoon alone – his wife was visiting her sick sister. His house was only a couple of blocks away. He was lonely.

"You're an awfully good-looking girl."

Betty set her elbows on the top of the bench and leaned back. "Yeah, God's been good."

"Mm hm." Pause. "Would you like to visit me at my place?"

"Oh, I don't know."

"I'd make worth your while."

"I don't know."

"Twenty?"

Betty was enjoying herself, really enjoying herself for the first time in her life.

Later, when she returned to the manse, Reverend Phil was on the phone in a polite confrontation with Page High's drama authority Mrs Sherman. The latter had announced that her annual play would be performed on Christmas Eve, due to the fact that it had religious overtones. The Reverend objected, reminding Mrs Sherman that the Page Methodist Church always had its Nativity pageant on Christmas Eve, and that there would even be "shepherds" in his pageant who were a part of Mrs Sherman's large cast. Cajoling and flattering, the Reverend finally convinced Mrs Sherman to present her epic after the New Year, perhaps on Epiphany.

He had never glanced at Betty while he was on the phone and now, after hanging up, he asked: "Where you been?" (The appellation "Sweetheart" was long gone.)

"I been out."

"Yeah? Where?"

"Out. I'm going to bed."

And she went to bed.

The Christmas pageant took a great deal of preparation, rehearsals and so forth. The holidays fell in the middle of the week, which meant that the amateur actors had to rehearse in the evenings, after they got off work. Joseph was played by a grocer clerk and Mary by a bank teller. Most of the other roles, shepherds and angels, were taken by students. The local undertaker Mr Simons, who had a stentorian voice, was going to narrate the story from St Luke, Chapter 2, with deletions and additions. It was Betty's responsibility to gather all the costumes and props needed for the pageant, but she had help from church ladies, who suggested bath robes for the shepherds and a faded gold evening gown from the Thirties for the main angel, set off by a tinsel halo. Matthew's magi, one in black face, were to stumble on dressed in left-over Halloween costumes, looking more like pirates than kings.

The angel's vintage evening gown was much too garish for a Heavenly messenger, an effect that had not been foreseen. The desert was suggested by cacti and succulents, and candles took the place of stars.

The performance went fairly well, primarily because the actors had no lines to speak. Mary almost dropped the Son of God when she tripped on the altar steps, revealing him to be a cute plastic baby doll with blinking eyes. And Joseph's terry-cloth turban kept coming loose so that he had to keep pushing it back into place.

The pantomime was only about twenty minutes long, but it was followed by Reverend Phil's sermon, which droned on for another forty-five minutes, deploring the evils of modern life. Avoid drinking! Avoid frivolous entertainment! Above all, avoid thinking!

Later that night there was a quiet supper at the manse. Tony was invited over and whispered *sotto voce* to his sister: "No champagne?" She only gave him a sour smile, along with a glass of flat cider. Dickie caught that exchange.

And here must be revealed a secret: Elizabeth and Anthony Dawson were not really prohibitionists. They had attended the Don't Drink rally to support an unhappy friend of Tony's who was considering Alcoholics Anonymous and had hoped to find support in the abstemious Christian community. Once Reverend Phil had made his assumption they did not disillusion him, as they saw him as a rock of security in their intestate lives.

The next day was Christmas and Reverend Phil had a morning sermon to deliver, very much the same sermon he had inflicted on his congregation after the pageant. Betty sat stiffly in the front row, smiled and wished holiday greetings, then got in the car and drove to the capital. Howie's was decorated with red and green streamers, a glowing tree slumped in the corner, and a hillbilly version of "Silent Night" whined on the juke box. After a couple of beers, ignoring the attentions of an inebriated farm hand, Betty left the bar.

Sitting on a bench in the square, she pulled her jacket about her and stared into space. The square was empty but after a few minutes a tall black Marine appeared and said "Merry Christmas", a phrase which she repeated.

"All alone?" he asked, and she nodded.

He didn't dare sit beside her (he could have gone to prison!), but he stood before her, introducing himself as Moses from Camp Lejeune and told her he was far from home and staying at his friend Jake's house on the Southern side of town. "It's a shame to be alone on Christmas day," he smiled, looking off into the distance. "Guess I walked too far. The bus service sure is slow on a holiday."

Betty sat forward. "I got a car. You need a ride back to your friend's house?"

"Why, that'd be right nice of you, ma'am."

So Betty drove the Marine back to his friend's house and spent two hours drinking beer and whiskey with Moses and Jake, both handsome boys.

She got back to the manse around five in the afternoon. Reverend Phil was waiting for her.

"Where you been?"

"The North Pole. I had a ball."

He pulled off his glasses and stuck out his nose. "You been drinking?"

"I had an egg nog with Santa."

"I got things for you to do."

"Later. I gotta see to Gritz."

The ball game had ended, the sound was off, and a vague comedy was flickering on the screen. Gritz was lying on his bed. Betty turned off the picture and said: "Gritz, you okay?"

"My back aches something terrible."

"I can get you a hot water bottle."

"Naw, naw. Get me a beer, will ya?"

"Sure." Betty went to the small refrigerator. Gritz called over: "Get yourself one too."

"Oh, thanks, Gritz. God, what a day!" She opened two beers and brought them over to the bed. Gritz had propped himself up with pillows.

They clinked bottles. Betty said "Merry Christmas."

"Merry bull," Gritz answered, causing Betty to laugh. Then she looked closer. "Gritz, are you okay?"

"Oh, yeah, I'm okay. I'm tired as hell and my back hurts, but I'm okay."

When she had finished her beer she went back upstairs. "Gritz is complaining of feeling bad, Phil. He doesn't look well."

"Ah, he's always complaining. Come on, Tony's here, let's have supper. Then we got some typing to do."

Dinner blessings were getting longer and longer. This Christmas night the blessing lasted twenty minutes while Reverend Phil thanked God for everything but the Spanish Inquisition. Betty and Tony glanced back and forth. Dickie stared ahead, planning.

New Year's Eve came and went with ginger ale and jeremiads about the new era. Reverend Phil had promised Mrs Sherman all his support for her annual play if she would present it after his Christmas Eve pageant, so when she suggested the first Sunday in January he agreed and more or less ordered his flock to attend if they wanted to avoid hellfire. "It'll be a beautiful show, oh yes, a beautiful show all about the early Christians. You all go see it!"

Mrs Sherman's father had bequeathed her a trunk load of books and there, amidst the obscure Victorian fiction and Fanny Farmer recipes, she discovered a copy of Stange's dramatization of "Quo Vadis?", and she decided to produce this spectacle in the Page High auditorium, despite the obvious physical difficulties. The auditorium's stage did not exactly rival the Bolshoi and there was no backstage. There was a basement, and that's where the sets had to be stored. Mrs Sherman's "football boys" carried the Appian Way, the SPQR, and the arena of martyrdom up the basement stairs onto the stage, scene by scene. As for the cast (dressed in ill-fitting costumes from a rental agency), the Homecoming Queen Ellen McSward played Lygia and the role of Vinicius, of course, was assumed by the wooden Benjamin Cowper. Nero was portrayed by an overweight overbearing boy in a wheelchair. Needless to say, he could not manage entrances and exits, so blocking had to be worked around him till the curtains closed and fullbacks lugged up the next décor. The burning of Rome was suggested by a great deal of dry ice and red flashing lights, accompanied by offstage screaming.

Reverend Phil escorted Betty, Tony, and Dickie to the eight o'clock performance. Admission price was one dollar fifty with open seating. Throughout the play Betty and Tony kept secretly and hilariously nudging each other, while Dickie simply disappeared after Act I. This laborious production, what with the long scene changes, lasted till nearly midnight, and when it was finally over Reverend Phil pronounced it "Inspiring! Really beautiful!"

Principal Cowper was also in the audience, enjoying and applauding his son's heroic performance, but as soon as the play was over he had to hurry home and get some sleep. The next day was Monday. Only a few of the cast members had congratulatory hot dogs and Cokes at Roy's before they went home.

As for Principal Skip, he had some important business in the capital: the rat fiasco from last September was not forgotten, and Skip had to appear before the Board of Health in the capital's City Hall. There the principal sat in a large room at a large desk before a judge and a court reporter, supported by Vice Principal Faber, the school's dietician, Clyde the cook, and the Lassiter boy, the Siegfried who had actually cornered and killed the dragon.

"Mr Faber, what is your opinion of the Page school in general?"

"Judge, it's one of the finest schools I've ever worked in. An excellent school, Sir."

"And, Larry, exactly how did you kill the rat?"

"Sir, I done picked up a chair and thrown it."

"Mrs Murray, are all health regulations carried out in the kitchen? I mean fully?"

"Oh, yes, Sir, absolutely."

"And, Clyde, have you had any more sightings of rats or any other vermin?"

"Nawsir, maybe an ant or two. That there rat was unusual, <u>really</u> unusual. Rare-like."

"Principal Cowper ... "

"Yessir?"

"Okay, this will have to be written up, of course, and it will mean a demerit for Page High. Any incident of this nature must never happen again. It could mean the closing of Page. Do you understand?"

"Oh, yessir. Yes, I understand. Thank you. Thank all of you. Oh, and thank the mayor."

With that the case was closed and Principal Cowper invited his supporters to lunch in a fancy restaurant downtown. Not Clyde, of course, but he received a slap on the back and was called "a good boy". As for Larry, he had never been in a restaurant before and had difficulty dealing with the various utensils, not to mention à la carte.

From then on Principal Cowper took personal control of the cafeteria, assigning various teachers as daily overseers. The colored staff was terrified lest Coach Kickoff be assigned to kitchen detail, eager to establish his physical authority. Skip decided the menu should be enlarged – "make it, you know, more homey" – so he had Mrs Murray introduce soupy spaghettis and brick-dry meat loafs to the bill of fare, and to support these enhancements the lunch price was raised thirty cents.

At the manse Gritz had pretty much given up eating. Betty would bring down biscuits and gravy, but Gritz would only ask for another beer ("Dang, I hurt. Oh, Honey, I really hurt!") so Betty would take a couple of beers from the refrigerator and eat the biscuits and gravy herself. She was developing quite an appetite.

"Phil," she would say, "Gritz isn't eating and he says he doesn't feel well,"

"Oh, he's okay. Let him be."

"But he's complaining about his back and his arm. He says — "

"Oh, he's always saying. He's always been a complainer. Let him be."

"Maybe he should see Dr Tobin or go to the clinic at King's."

"Maybe you should be his nurse. Stop going down there so much. Let him be."

But almost two weeks into the New Year one evening Betty took some popcorn down to Gritz and found him lying on the floor. There was a stench in the room. Kneeling beside Gritz, Betty realized he was very still and his stare was fixed. Hurrying back upstairs, she went into the puce-painted den and whispered: "Gritz is dead."

Reverend Phil pulled off his eyeglasses, looked her over, then said "Are you sure?"

"Oh, yes, it's obvious."

"Jeepers."

"Well, is that all you have to say? We have to call Dr Tobin."

"Well, then go ahead and call him. Jeepers, this time of night!"

The doctor came over, pronounced the patient dead, diagnosed a myocardial infarction, and called the coroner. "No, no, Mack, clear M.I.. Yep, yep. He's Reverend Phil's brother. You know Reverend Phil. His brother. Yep, yep. Oh, <u>yep</u>!" Low laugh.

Mr Simons of Sleepy Time Funeral Home supervised the interment at Page Sweet Peace Cemetery on the outskirts of town. The funeral, of course, was held at the Page Methodist Church, Reverend Philip Fairfield presiding, the ceremony open casket so that everyone could see what a corpse looks like. White roses and Queen Anne's Lace. After wiping his cheeks ostentatiously with his pocket handkerchief, Reverend Phil approached the pulpit and blinked out at the congregation, two-thirds of which barely knew the deceased. "I guess, I guess our Lord Jesus got lonely up there in his Heaven and needed a good

Christian man to keep him company, so he called our brother George. He couldn't ask for better company! I'll bet old George is up there right now swapping stories with St Peter."

A strain of subdued sympathetic laughter.

"George and I were the only children our dear parents had, and we were always so close, so close. We always looked after each other and cared for each other so much."

At this point Betty, dressed in black, rose from the pew and hurried into the vestibule. Dickie and Tony looked at each other, then Tony slowly shook his head. Reverend Phil had not even noticed.

"Now we have to say Goodby to our good honest George and send him to his well-deserved rest. We'll always think of you, dear brother, and remember your faithful soul, which is safe in our Father's Paradise."

In the vestibule Betty was kneeling by a table, clutching one of its legs. The cramp had started abruptly and she had come close to crying out, right there in the chapel. It was the second one she had had since dawn and it left her damp and slightly nauseous. Two mornings before she had raced to the bath room when she felt her coffee coming up; now she felt she might throw up again. She couldn't go back to the chapel; she would meet them outside. Could she make it through the ceremony at the Page Sweet Rest Cemetery? She had to try. Her mind was racing a mile a minute. She had missed her last "crucifixion" and now she was experiencing all sorts of uncomfortable symptoms. Her most recent encounter with the Reverend had been on Christmas Eve after the success of his tableau and of course he assumed he had consummated his dedication. He may have, and that was Betty's gamble. Reverend Phil had probably seen the encounter as a crusade and God's Will had triumphed. Let him believe that, and it would be safe to go to Dr Tobin with an aura of divine expectancy. "Oh, Doctor, I think, I'm not certain, but … "

Rebecca of Sunnybrook Farce.

As it turned out Dr Tobin referred her to a gynecologist in the capital, an earnest young man with a chirpy receptionist and a maternal nurse. He took a blood test and told her he would contact her in a few days. When he did call back he was exuberant: "Guess what, Mrs Fairfield? You're going to be a mama!"

Betty: "Oh … thanks, Doctor. Yeah, thanks."

The following Sunday Reverend Phil approached the pulpit rubbing his hands and grinning like that cat from Cheshire. "Oh, my dear friends, I have wonderful news, wonderful beautiful news. My little girl Betty is going to be a mother. Yes, she and I have begot a child." Oos and Ahs from his congregation. "I am so proud and so thankful to our good Lord for this blessing and I wanted all our good friends at the church to be the first to know."

After that Betty became the object of concern and compassion from women she didn't really know. She had to put up with matrons approaching with remarks such as "And how's that little iddle-widdle? Aren't babies <u>wonderful</u>?"

"Sure." Betty was dealing with heaviness, fatigue, and a peanut butter fixation. All she needed was someone telling her how wonderful the iddle-widdle was.

Easter fell in late March and Betty was responsible for preparing the Methodist Sunday School Easter egg hunt. In the dead of night she and Tony crept around the church yard, hiding decaled parti-colored hardboiled eggs in hedges and under drain pipes, the prize egg the golden egg itself placed far under one of the back steps of the chapel. The discovery of that egg won the finder a crisp five dollar bill. It would be nice to say that the children were calmly competitive during this post-sermon game, but alas! they were combative in the most unchristian manner, the result being torn and dirtied best and even a bloody nose. Two children stared at Betty's tumescence, then raced away giggling.

Easter was always economic season for Reverend Phil, something to do with resurrection, and the morning sermon's topic was "The Widow's Mite, and What it Means to Page". To one side of the altar, backed by a spray of calla lilies, was a large drawing executed by Shirley Lee Shawnsee depicting a ragged woman leading with her left hand a hollowed-eyed little girl while with her right she dropped her last farthing into a treasury box outside a house of worship.

"Our good Lord told his disciples that the poor widow's mite meant more to God than the rich man's contributions because it was all she had, her last coin. So our Lord God knows that when we give a ten percent – a <u>mere</u> ten percent of our blessings to the church it means that the beautiful teachings of Jesus Christ can be spread to poor sufferers. Give! Give in the name of God!"

Pledge cards of tithing were handed out. Of course, a flicker of thought may have made one wonder why the poor widow didn't buy her obviously starving daughter some bread with her last coin. And Mr Webber, manager of a hardware concern, might have questioned why his $500.00 should go to the church rather than be spent on his family's food, clothes, and car fuel.

It was in April, shortly after Easter, that Betty began arranging and re-arranging the basement apartment, cleaning and stocking, or at least supervising Mandy to do so: the maid saw to it that the studio was painted. A new "sight-sound thing" (this one with color) was installed along with a new couch and arm chair. The bookshelves, always empty during Gritz's stay, would soon be crammed with volumes both heavy and light, also long-playing records of Ellington, Brubeck, and Parker. Mandy handled all the necessary lifting and pushing (for an extra ten dollars) because of course Betty had difficulty getting up and down the stairs. The reason for this renovation: she and Tony had decided that he could move in sometime in late April. Reverend Phil was given an ultimatum and had to agree, accepting the $100.00 rent fee. What the Reverend didn't know was that Tony would not always be alone.

One night in the campus Rathskeller he had met his future girl-friend, Myrna by name, a blonde who not only had a pin up figure, she had a 1955 Buick Roadmaster convertible, a gift from her father on her

21st birthday. Myrna was not a student but worked part-time in a lawyer's office in the capital, that lawyer being one her father's colleagues.

When asked by the reverend what he would be doing over the summer months, Tony answered: "Dolce far niente."

And so springtime went on. At Page High the baseball season had begun, but Coach Templar proved no more victorious at America's favorite pastime as he had at football, shortstop Arnold Miller notwithstanding. The baseball team the Page Eagles lost game after game.

Because of, not in spite of, his intimidating presence Coach Templar was appointed hall monitor between certain periods. His red-faced fury could come rushing out of nowhere at the hint of a misdemeanor, be it calling out too loud or leaving a locker door open. The recalcitrant could be pushed against a wall, kicked, or even slapped across the side of the head. If any other authority figure complained Principal Cowper would smile "Oh, yeah, that's our coach. He keeps 'em in shape."

A slight scandal occurred when Lottie Haymaker had to drop out of school and it was whispered she was "in trouble". Things got worse when she named a teammate of Arnold's as the source of her inconvenience. But that gallant, Sullivan by name, said he knew three other boys who had been "behind the box cars" with Lottie also, thus blunting Lottie's claims for paternity. One of those implicated was Benjamin Cowper, so the whole thing was swept under the carpet and Lottie left town temporarily to visit relatives.

To counteract this disgrace Miss Farro announced in April she had found Her Own True Love. It wasn't a French duke or a motorcycle daredevil, it was a thirtyish accountant she met at the Baptist Church Bible Picnic. They had been comparing ideas on contrition and it happened: somewhere between the potato salad and the pineapple upside-down cake they had fallen head over heels. Wedding plans were pending, perhaps December.

It was also in April that Mr Nelson stopped Dickie in a corridor one afternoon and said: "Dickie, I understand you're interested in playing drums in our band. Or at least Miss Farro told me a while back you were interested. Why don't you join us? You know, Jeff Morgan's going to be graduating in May and we'll be needing a new drummer. How about it?"

So Dickie went to the school's rehearsal hall and began taking instructions from Mr Nelson and Jeff Morgan on how to properly handle the drums. Left to his own devices he propped himself behind the set and began tearing, beating into incorrigible rhythms.

"Hey hey, Dickie, we're not Gene Krupa here! We'll do it slow and easy, the way Jeff showed ya." So much for Dickie's membership in the Page High band. He never spoke to Mr Nelson again.

Commencement exercises were held in the same auditorium where "Quo Vadis?" had triumphed, but Vice Principal Faber didn't ask the graduating students whither they were going but rather to be patriotic and God-fearing whitherever. Whatever path they were to take, they were to avoid that darn godless Communism, scourge of the free world. Always trust in Democracy and God, and your life can never go wrong. <u>God</u> bless America, boys and girls. Amen.

Spring melted away and summer came to Page. Swimming parties at Edwin Park in the capital – there were no private pools in Page – roller skating parties, movie parties, slumber parties, card parties, and of course Bible study parties. Baseball or croquet. There was even a book club, where one could digest the intricacies of Thomas B Costain. No Balzac. No Faulkner. Those names were unknown in the Page Eager Reader Book Club.

Some enthusiasts left town for a couple of weeks to visit Grand Canyon or Yellowstone National Park, returning with stacks of grinning photographs and colorful tales of sunsets and bears.

One late afternoon in late August Betty came to the door of the den, where Reverend Phil was staring at his sermon. "I need help," she said.

"Mm. Mandy's out."

"Not that kind of help. I should be in the hospital."

"Oh! Now?"

She was standing there with a towel in one hand and her overnight case in the other. "Yes. Now."

Neither spoke a word during the drive to King's Hospital in the capital. They parked the car in the ambulance entrance and hurried into Reception; Betty was taken upstairs while the Reverend did the paper work. Afterward he went to the third floor where he waited a half an hour before a nurse came out and told him "You might as well go home, Mr Fairfield. Nothing's going to happen for a while."

"Reverend."

"That's okay. The doctor's been called. He's coming in. It'll be a while. You go on home."

Reverend Phil returned to the manse where he slept off and on. Mandy made some supper which he barely touched. Finally he put on his bath robe (Joseph's coat in the Christmas pageant) and lay down in bed. It was shortly after six thirty in the morning when the phone rang; it was the maternity ward telling him a boy had been born. Feverish with excitement, he pulled on some clothes, pulled on his eye glasses, and pushed himself into the Ford, reaching the parking lot at King's twenty minutes later. The main entrance was locked, so he entered the Emergency Room, identifying himself to the night shift. The nurse paused. "Oh. Oh, yes. I'll page Mrs Schramm."

"Who's Mrs Schramm?"

"She's the night supervisor. She'll escort you to the maternity ward."

"Is something wrong?"

"Wrong? Oh, no. No. She'll take you there."

Mrs Schramm arrived, as pale and starchy as her cap. "Mr Fairfield?"

"Reverend Fairfield."

"Oh, Reverend. Oh." She turned to the young nurse who was with her. "Well. Well, Sonya, let's take Mr Fairfield up."

Sonya barely whispered: "Yes ma'am."

"Is something wrong?"

"Well, no, Mr Fairfield. Come with us."

He followed the two nurses to a back elevator which took them to the third floor and a dimly-lit corridor. "This way, Mr Fairfield."

"Reverend!"

The supervisor stopped at a room, door ajar.

"Stay here, Sonya." Then Mrs Schramm led Reverend Phil into the obscure room, flicked on a soft light, and there was the baby, dark as the end of day, with black frizzled hair and large chocolate eyes.

Reverend Phil immediately turned away. "You've made a mistake."

"No, Mr Fairfield, this is the baby that was delivered at five fifty-three this morning."

"But it's not mine. You must have a woman – a woman of color here. This is her child."

"No, Sir, all patients – patients of color are at Shaw's across town."

"But this baby – this baby is not mine."

"Sir, this baby was delivered at five fifty-three this morning. Now, if — "

"Are you BLIND? Are you INSANE? This baby is a NEGRO!"

Calmly: "Sonya, have the desk call Security."

"Call Security! Call City Hall! This baby is not mine!"

"Mr Fairfield — "

"REVEREND!"

Overhead: "Security, Third Floor Maternity. Security, Third Floor Maternity."

"Reverend, perhaps you should speak to Dr Atherton. He'll help you understand — "

"Lady, Dr Schweitzer couldn't help me understand how you could – you could —"

A beefy redhead in uniform appeared. "Mrs Schramm?"

"Oh, Ray, Mr Fairfield's been a little upset, but I think he's calming down now. I believe he wants to talk with Dr Atherton."

"No, I don't want to talk with Dr Atherton. I want to see my wife."

"All right. Now, Sir, she may be a little weak." Mrs Schramm and Ray led Reverend Phil around a corner and to Room 310. Mrs Schramm held up her hand. "Now let me check." She cracked the door open, whispered: "Mrs Fairfield?"

A bright "Yes?"

"Your husband's here."

"Oh, wonderful! Please show him in."

Mrs Schramm stood back and held the door open, giving Ray a subtle nod. After Reverend Phil had entered, she closed the door.

There was Betty, propped up, not at all weak, dark hair swept back from her forehead, no makeup, wearing a serious smile. "Have you seen the baby?"

Reverend Phil sat in a chair near the edge of the bed. "Yes, yes, I've seen the baby."

"Isn't he beautiful? I can't wait to take him home."

"Betty, we can't take that thing to the manse."

"That thing? That's my baby. I'm going to take him home and raise him. I fell in love with him the second I saw him."

Reverend Phil dropped to the floor on his knees, his hands folded beneath his chin, his lips moving tremulously.

"Stop that! Stop it!"

"Oh, Lord Jesus, merciful Lord Jesus! Who is the father?"

"Are you talking to me?" Betty screwed up her mouth. "I, actually I'm not sure."

"Oh, God! Oh, God Jesus!"

"Shut up! Get off the floor, get up!"

He got up and sat down. "What are we going to do?"

Betty folded her hands and looked at him. "It's easy. We'll tell people my baby was stillborn. I was grief stricken, and then I heard about this little brown baby that had been abandoned here at the emergency room and I (in the great goodness of my heart) decided to raise that baby as my own. Everybody will love me for it."

"But the hospital … ?"

"The church will give King's a big donation."

"Well, yeah … I guess we could. But … but the congregation?

Betty stared at him. "The congregation? Phil, you could tell them the sun rises in the West and they'd believe you. They're stupid."

And so it came to pass. Betty named the child Justice and took him to the manse where he was to be raised. The spare room became the nursery and Betty moved in there, setting up her bed right next to the cradle. Though slender and not particularly bossy, Mandy proved an excellent mammy, helping with diapers and bottles. Tony's friend Myrna began visiting more and more often, leaving (to Reverend Phil's consternation) her Buick convertible parked out front. Far from being spoiled, Myrna was sympathetic and supportive; she and Betty became friends, decorating Tony's basement apartment with ukiyo-e prints and a shoji screen which hid the bed. Betty spent evenings with Tony and Myrna, sharing their spaghetti meals including chianti and light jazz. Justice joined them at the dining table in a high chair.

Reverend Phil told his congregation the story just as Betty had narrated it to him. The "brown baby" had been adopted by Betty out of compassion and was to be raised as a family member. What a shame she had lost her own child, but we can't question the ways of the Good Lord. And, as Betty had predicted, the parishioners told each other they believed the story. But, as Matthew says, some doubted.

The Page Methodist Church donated (from the tithing fund) $5,000.00 to King's Hospital in the capital "in recognition of the compassionate support given during my wife's difficulty". The donation was used for surgical additions, while medical records (including birth certificates) were strategically altered. When the earnest young gynecologist began asking questions he was told in so many words by the hospital administration to shut up.

It was about this time that Dickie disappeared, forsaking his Senior year at Page High. And it was realized when the deduction was made from the tithing fund that $300.00 had also been taken, shortly before Dickie disappeared. They found a type-written note from the boy: *Don't look for me.* And, considering the note, they thought it best not to look for him.

He traveled West. Hiking, hitch-hiking, he came to rest 500 miles away in Nashville, where he attended the fair in Centennial Park and slept among the columns of the modern Parthenon. Eating hot dogs and beans he wandered about the city, wondering what to do next. He met a group of people his own age and was encouraged to join them at the Ryman Auditorium concert. "You'll love the music!" But he didn't; he found the music sentimental and quaint and decided to leave town.

Crossing the Cumberland River he moved further West. A good-natured family was headed towards Santa Fe and he joined them. Santa Fe, with its adobe and artistic atmosphere, appealed to him and he stayed on. He found a job hauling trash and stayed in a warehouse cubicle. On one of his free days he went hiking and wound up in Alto Park near the river. He was dozing on a bench when he was joined by an elderly man, out strolling, who invited Dickie to a Mexican restaurant downtown. Guacamole and enchiladas. The old gentleman sneaked Dickie a Margarita and told him how sad it was the opera season had ended, the perfect entertainment for a sensitive young lad. But the gentleman himself had a wall full of long-playing records and would love to expose his new friend to the glories of Puccini. Wouldn't Dickie like to come home with him? During coffee Dickie excused himself and vanished, thus evading both the attentions of his host and the lamentations of Cio-Cio-San.

A few days later he left Santa Fe forever. Once again he attached himself to another family that was traveling further West, this time twice the distance, planning to stop in Las Vegas for some fun. That vivacious city of lurid flashing lights fascinated Dickie, with its acre-long casinos, its film celebrities appearing live on stage, its aura of never-sleeping never-ending energy, and its careless economic attitudes.

Dickie found work in a 24-hour coffee shop covering a night shift dressed in a starched white shirt and a little white paper cap. The shop's pièce de résistance was the Midnight Burger, which consisted of a thick charcoaled patty, sliced onion, chopped jalapeño, chili mustard, pimento cheese, lettuce and tomato on a caraway bun. A blonde middle-aged divorcée dressed décolleté was addicted to the Midnight Burger (as well as the slot machines) and she frequented the coffee shop around one. She always sat in a booth, brought her own gin-tonics, and left ten-, twenty-dollar tips.

She displayed a great interest in Dickie and naturally asked him about his life in Vegas. Discovering that he got off work at seven, she invited him to her room right there in the hotel. A few mornings later she invited him to her ranch-style house with swimming pool on the outskirts of town. She would drive him back and forth in her pink Chrysler coupe to and from work, never leaving the casino during his shift.

This relationship lasted till Dickie met an older man (yes, in the coffee shop) who was interested in Dickie but only as a driver who could help the gentleman get back to his house and family in Santa Rosa. The state of California also appealed to Dickie and so he accepted the offer to be a chauffeur, leaving his patroness to her décolleté clothes, her swimming pool, and her slot machines. Dickie's place in the coffee shop, and in the divorcée's heart, was taken by a rugged twenty-two year old of Cherokee heritage, hoping to find employment as a dealer.

The trip to Santa Rosa in a rented car was a little over 600 miles, Dickie's employer sleeping most of the way, but a steak breakfast and a steak dinner were paid for.

Santa Rosa was a bustling friendly town and Dickie was invited to stay with his host, the wife and two kids. There was a space over the garage, and he filled in as their temporary handyman. The businessman and his wife were of an earlier era, and their musical appreciation reflected the Big Band rhythms which they introduced to Dickie. "I like drums," Dickie told them. "I like 'em fast and loud. I'd like to play in a band."

"Well, you should be in San Francisco," Madame decided, and her husband agreed.

And so it happened that after a couple of weeks he (with the help of his new friends) moved 55 miles South and settled in a section of the City near the park, where he got a job in a somewhat crummy burger joint and began evenings going to coffee houses, reading philosophy and talking to unhappy dissidents. People became aware of his interests, and he was invited to join a musical group where he was featured as their lead drummer. At first people complained his playing was a little aggressive, but slowly they began to appreciate his style and the club where he played became increasingly crowded. "You oughta <u>hear</u> him!" Even the musicians he played with could be a little alarmed and there were nights when they just stopped, stood back and stared in astonished, admiring disbelief.

Over the years Dickie's appearance changed. He cut his hair in a Mohawk, sometimes orange, sometimes mint, and wore faded pullovers and ragged jeans. His tattoos included a tarantula, a dark shrouded figure holding a hatchet, and an empty cross dripping blood.

He called himself Demon.

ELEANOR PACKARD

IT WAS NOT A HAPPY MARRIAGE. MARVIN LEE PACKARD and his bride, the former Patty Brown, both born in 1914, were high school sweethearts, the games, the prom, the courtship. Their wedding took place in the summer 0f 1932, a month after graduation, and the couple spent a week in Manhattan for their honeymoon, sponsored by the parents, staying at the New Yorker, seeing "The Cat and the Fiddle" and traveling into the Bronx to watch the Yankees beat St Louis. It was, alas, on this honeymoon that Marvin Lee learned that he and his bride were not totally compatible, something the mores of the time denied him learning during the courtship.

On returning home they settled into the five-room rent-free cottage on Mr Brown's property, a half-mile from downtown, and (this time with Mr Packard's sponsorship) Marvin Lee became a candy salesman, representing the Rite-Sweet Wholesale Company which catered to the lobbies of hotels and movie theaters, while Patty settled into a routine of domestic supervision. She was responsible for buying the groceries, based on Marvin Lee's 75¢ an hour, plus commissions, depending on how many Baby Ruths he sold to the Midtown Hotel or the Star Cinema.

Marvin Lee was gregarious and good-natured (towards other men) and took to the life of a candy drummer with confidence, sometimes (despite his youth) joining the other salesmen for cigars and shots of whiskey. The shots and cigars became more frequent over time following his marriage and Marvin Lee did not like being cautioned about his habits, either by his wife or his father-in-law, the latter becoming increasingly inquisitorial.

"Daddy says," Patty would begin, and what followed would be one of Daddy's complaints or criticisms regarding Marvin Lee and/or his companions.

"Yeah, he says. Just leave me alone!"

Often Marvin Lee would go out at night, leaving his wife alone with the company of the comedic radio. There were times he didn't come back to the cottage till early morning, resulting in silences and resentful stares.

It was remarkable how quickly this impasse evolved and equally remarkable was Patty's announcement in the midst of the gridlock that she was with child. Had she conceived in the suite of the New Yorker? Perhaps, but now, as they say, the honeymoon was over.

Patty did not bear well. The months ahead were ones of impatient torment, and Marvin Lee despised her discomfort and loathed her maternal instinct, the innate authority.

It was a contentious winter, Patty being catered to by her mother and Mrs Packard, while Marvin Lee sold chocolates and drank Old Crow. He and Mr Brown had begun arguing.

The child was born shortly after three in the morning on April 1st with Mr Brown, Mr Packard and Marvin Lee smoking in the hospital's newly-painted (peach) waiting room. Dr Cachot himself came out to assure them the delivery was healthy and the mother was fine. It was a girl, crying of course, crying piteously as though she resented coming into the world.

"Unhappy!" the doctor smiled.

It had been decided it was going to be a boy and was to be named Franklin, after the new President; but it wasn't a boy it was a girl and so was named Eleanor, after the new First Lady.

Marvin Lee felt cheated.

The girl was taken to the cottage where a storage room had been transformed into a nursery, Patty herself (dressed in slacks, her hair in a snood) hanging the clown-crowded wallpaper and painting the shelves pink. Marvin Lee ignored the place and the child, who, over the next two years, rapidly grew into a pretty little girl with auburn hair, light blue eyes and freckles. Those two years were a period of disturbed desperation, the marriage freezing. Affable and good-looking in a bucolic sort of way, Marvin Lee had an assortment of friends, male and female, most of whom Patty, like her mother not sociable, knew nothing about. He rarely made it home for dinner, sometimes not for breakfast. But one chill September evening, having spent all afternoon with a purveyor of neck ties and that worthy's girlfriend, Marvin Lee staggered in early and, surprising his wife in her slip, took on the role of alert husband, despite Patty's protestations. It was discovered later that she was once again expecting, at which point Marvin Lee jammed his finger in her gaze and snarled "This one better be a boy!"

His threat came true: in June of the following year, following Eleanor's third birthday, Patty suffered through the birth of a boy that Marvin Lee proudly named James, or Jim.

The boy became the Adam's apple of his father's eye. Even while it was still an infant Marvin Lee would carry it to the offices of the Rite-Sweet Wholesale Company, extolling its strength, its intelligence, the beauty of its red hair and blue eyes. "Look at those hands – what a pitcher he'll make!" or "My boy's going to really shock the girls, you'll see!"

It was always "my boy", never "ours"; it was as though the child had sprung from the father's forehead, a leader of men. The mother was good for toilet training and changing diapers, but the boy's life was <u>his</u>, the father's. It was Marvin Lee who held Jim's arms when the child was learning to walk, and of course the boy's first word was Da.

After Jim had learned to talk Marvin Lee taught him how to mock his mother and sister, calling them the dumb girls, the stupid sissies.

He ordered Eleanor's room re-painted dark blue, the clowns replaced by images of Robin Hood and his Merry Men, standing tall while shooting arrows or seated spread-legged while drinking mead. Eleanor herself was relegated to a closet-like space adjacent to the garage where Marvin Lee parked the jalopy mandatory for his sales peregrinations.

For his son's third birthday Marvin Lee ordered a picnic at the Jolly Time Amusement Park, located outside town, where there was a picnic area including swings, a sliding board, and an unguarded pool. Marvin Lee told Patty to watch the kids so that he could join some strangers at the beer station near a minature Ferris wheel. It was a warm day; Marvin Lee was thirsty. He was in the midst of a long-winded drummer yarn when the group heard cries and screams coming from the play area. Several people had rushed toward the pool.

Marvin Lee broke off his anecdote with a "What th' hell?" before he heard a woman's voice calling out "Oh, no, it's a little boy!"

An alarm went off inside the father and, tipping over his Acme beer bottle, he raced from his companions across the playground towards the crowd that had gathered around the pool.

Someone had dragged Jim from the water, his thick wet red hair splayed across his forehead, and a youth wearing swim trunks was kneeling over the child's body, carefully crossing and pressing his hands under the sternum with all the expertise of a Boy Scout, which is what the youth was. He looked up sharply: "Is there a doctor here?"

By this time Marvin Lee had rushed up and fell to his knees by his son.

"Are you a doctor, Sir?"

"I'm his father."

"Oh. I'm trying, Sir. An ambulance has been called, and the police. I'm afraid, Sir … "

"Oh, God," Marvin Lee whispered. He heard a scream behind him. It was Patty, clutching Eleanor against her side, the girl staring at her brother. Marvin regarded them only for a moment, then looked back at his son's cyanotic face. "Oh, God!"

The medics arrived shortly before the police car, listened to the Boy Scout's story, as they worked frantically. After a few minutes they stood up and stepped back, the leader shaking his head at one of the cops. By this time Marvin Lee was sobbing.

Another officer knelt by Marvin Lee and told him the boy would have to be taken to the hospital so he could be examined and pronounced by a doctor. The father nodded and, staggering up, began to walk away as the medics retrieved a gurney from the ambulance. Marvin Lee didn't even glance at his wife or daughter, just reached over briefly and pressed the Boy Scout's shoulder, then followed the cops to their car. The police felt Marvin Lee should not try to drive, so a third officer followed the car in Marvin Lee's jalopy. Patty and Eleanor were left standing by the pool, the mother deciding the only thing to do was to go to her parents, where she and Eleanor would stay until the funeral. They caught a bus outside the Jolly Time Amusement Park.

The four grand-parents shared the expense of the small cream-colored coffin, bickering the entire time about who was at fault for the tragedy.

The funeral was held in Mrs Brown's church, Marvin Lee stone cold, many people crying only because it was the death of a child. Jim was buried in a corner plot of a small cemetery, paid for by the grandparents, and after the ceremony, Patty was told she would have to go home.

It was night when she reached the cottage. Eleanor was sent to her small room, frightened, holding her only doll, a frowzy thing with dimples and golden curls. She could hear every word when the accusations started in the kitchen.

"Why th' hell weren't you watching him? I told you to watch him!"

"Me? Why weren't you watching him? No, you were too busy drinking beer with some other drunks!"

"Watch your mouth, almighty mama!'

"No! I tried, but I was watching Ellie."

"T'hell with Ellie! I wish it had <u>been</u> Ellie, you and Ellie both! You killed my son! You killed my son!"

"No, <u>you</u> killed your son, you damn drunkard!"

The resounding slap could be heard outside the cottage, and not for the first time. In her closet room Eleanor could hear the garage door yanked open and the jalopy roaring out into the night. Cautiously, she went into the kitchen where her mother, holding onto the sink, was pulling herself up off the floor and, turning on the tap, washing out her blood-dripping mouth.

"Mama?"

"Get out. Get back to your room <u>now</u>."

Marvin Lee never returned to the cottage. He sent his necktie friend to pick up his clothes and toiletries. "Marvin Lee's real sorry, Mrs Packard, he's a nice guy and all, he's just really upset about Jim."

"Mm." Patty helped the friend with the suitcase, the clothes, the cologne and razor blades, but barely said a word.

It became obvious that Marvin Lee had no intention of offering any more support. The Packards didn't care. Mr Brown would have pursued the matter but two months after his grand-son's death he himself was dead. He had suddenly lost his appetite and his energy, sank rapidly and died in mid-August, aged forty-seven. His wife became increasingly reclusive and was little help to their daughter. The cottage was still Patty's, but she had no income.

Taking a bus into town, she began looking for a job but her lack of experience made it difficult. Finally she found a job as an attendant at Williams' Cafeteria next to the Star Cinema. She took the same bus back and forth every day. One afternoon Marvin Lee saw her through the plate glass window cleaning off tables so he stopped going to Williams' Cafeteria for coffee.

It was Patty's mother who, uncomfortable with the two females living in a cottage without the male's overbearing presence, suggested that Patty adopt one of the puppies a next-door German Shepherd had littered,

Mrs Brown's neighbor lady having failed to have the dog "fixed", a common oversight at the time. "I can't afford it," Patty said, but Mrs Brown said her neighbor would help with the food, and Eleanor would be responsible for the dog. "It'll be good for her – she doesn't seem to have many friends." So the Shepherd was brought into the cottage and the backyard, where he spent a great deal of time. He became Eleanor's beloved pet and she named him, sensibly enough, Barker. It was the Widow Brown's only contribution before she followed her late husband.

As for Mr Packard, and therefore his wife, they made excuses for looking after Eleanor and kindergarten was out of the question, so the girl was left to her own devices. There was sometimes milk and food in the refrigerator and she was able to move back into her old room, now blue and medieval. There was an electrical outlet in one wall, so Eleanor plugged in the radio and listened to the soap operas, "Backstage Wife" and "Life Can Be Beautiful". Her favorite was "Pepper Young's Family" and she pretended to be Linda, acting out the role as the actress read her lines. She would dress in one of her mother's robes or scarves and emote as the facile drama unfolded, dancing across the floor or sitting demurely in a corner, Barker jumping around her. Often she would pretend she was in a movie version of the story.

As for Patty, she was so efficient and dependable, within a year she was promoted to supervisor at the cafeteria, making sure all the tables were clean and stable, all the trays clean and stacked. She had her lunch there and was allowed to take sandwiches or salads home with her, saving on groceries.

Patty's mother-in-law Mrs Packard at last saw to it that Eleanor was enrolled in school so she could learn to read and count, accomplishments that had never been hinted at by Patty. The fact is Patty barely knew how to read herself and had to be patiently taught cash register skills at Williams'. But she looked fresh and pretty in her green and white checked uniform and customers said she was the nicest employee there. One customer, Mr Sessums, assistant manager at the

Star Cinema, began casually courting Patty, bringing flowers to decorate the pastry counter and presenting passes to mother and daughter, Eleanor particularly enjoying the musicals. Mr Sessums, incidentally, had a wife and little boy.

Eleanor's first school year began. There was no school bus. Eleanor had to catch a city bus every morning (with her mother) to reach the Esther Light School which she attended, Esther Light being a philanthropist of the 19th Century, the wife of a general practitioner. Eleanor was a quick student, learning her letters and the multiplication table by the time she was seven. She also showed talent at drawing and impersonating celebrities. During her year at third grade it was decided the class would put on a small production of "Cinderella", and Eleanor was chosen to play the title role, gauzy dress, silver lamé bedroom slippers and all. Her Prince was Freddie Mercer, a blond future quarterback, and he was Eleanor's first crush. In fact, she thought there should be a kissing scene at the end, but Mrs Roman decided that holding hands and smiling was connubial enough, though she was impressed by Eleanor's performance. "Why, Ellie, you should be an actress!"

Eleanor was not that popular with the other girls: her mother couldn't afford pretty clothes or the multiple bracelets that were popular, and it was whispered Eleanor's father was a drunk who had beat his wife before he deserted her. ("Her mother's a waitress or something downtown!") Eleanor was generally not invited to parties or games and, because of what the students considered her degraded condition, she was sarcastically called Little Nell.

Her lack of inclusion would have been easier to accept if she had had a strong relationship with her mother, but she didn't. Patty would come home at night, usually tired and cross, then make dinner and listen to the radio while Eleanor did her home work in her room, which had remained dark blue though the Merry Men had been removed. Eleanor spent a great deal of time petting and training Barker. Mother and daughter had little to say to each other, little in common. Sometimes they would go to a movie, courtesy of Mr Sessums. Patty had learned he was married, but she was unaware that Rumor assumed that he was being favored for all those free entertainments. ("So ladylike in that little uniform! Butter wouldn't melt in her mouth!")

The coming of war changed their lives but little. Most of the men they knew were exempt (Patty heard that Marvin Lee was claiming to support a wife and child) and the food shortages, the rations made little difference in their meager routine. Patty worked in the cafeteria, now crowded with military uniforms, and Eleanor went to classes, now filled with little patriots, as they always had before.

It was during Eighth Grade that the real change came for Eleanor. In September of 1945, she complained of weakness and headaches, causing her to miss two days of school. Then one evening after homework she took an Evening in Paris bubble bath, a luxury Patty decided both she and her daughter could afford. After the bath she told her mother she felt really fatigued and that her legs were "tingly". Patty told her to go to bed and try to sleep, but when Eleanor awoke she found it was difficult to get out of bed. In fact she was partially paralyzed.

A doctor was called and after the examination he said "Well, Mrs Packard, I'm afraid your child has polio. She'll have to come to the hospital for a few days for further examination and the beginning of treatment. We have therapists and nurses who are specially trained."

Patty was alarmed. "But, Doctor, you don't mean that lung thing, that ..."

"The iron lung? No, I'm sure not. She doesn't seem to have any respiratory problems. These are muscular problems. She needs therapy and she may have to wear braces for a while."

"Braces?" Patty was thinking teeth.

The doctor perceived her misapprehension and said: "On her <u>legs</u>, Mrs Packard. You know, while she's learning to walk again. She tells me she can't stand up."

"But, Doctor, how much … I mean, I work in a cafeteria … "

"The Williams'. Yes, I've seen you there, Mrs Packard. No, the hospital has special plans and rates for polio patients. You can speak to the social worker tomorrow. I'm going to have ambulance attendants come tonight to take Eleanor to the hospital. Now, may I use your phone?"

As the doctor had prophesized, Eleanor was fitted with leg braces which were ugly and uncomfortable and at first required crutches. She did exercises every day with eight other children, including one with a grim imagination ("Gaw! I heard about this one boy he died after they chopped his legs off!") and often to the piano accompaniment of a popular inspirational song from a current Broadway show. The pianist even tried to sing the lyrics himself in an unstable tenor. After spending several sessions with the specialists, she was allowed to go back home to Patty's somewhat reluctant supervision. "She's doing splendidly, Mrs Packard, just follow our instructions."

The instructions included walking Eleanor around the cottage, first with the crutches, then with the braces only. Also therapeutic massaging, which Eleanor preferred done by a nurse. Eventually, after months, she could walk without the braces, holding onto a crutch. There was always the danger of a permanent limp, a prospect she dreaded.

The worst casualty of the illness was Barker. He was evicted from the cottage, doctor's orders.

Eleanor had missed a great deal of school time, and it was decided she could not return to the eighth grade after the first of the year, but would have to repeat the seventh grade, another degradation. One Sunday afternoon Eleanor rested on the couch while her mother did some light cleaning after lunch. When the phone rang Patty answered it. "Hello? Yes? Yes, this is Mrs Packard. Yes. Oh, yes? When? Oh … oh, I see. Well, of course. I see. Oh, well … thanks for calling. What? Mm."

After she hung up she turned to Eleanor and said "Your father is dead."

Pause. "Did he have an accident?"

"No. He just died. Cirrhosis."

Longer pause. "I never knew him."

"You were lucky."

Marvin Lee died, age 33, in the third-rate boarding house he had lived in for the past two years. His rigor mortis was discovered by an ageing woman of somber reputation when she woke up from a head-splitting sleep, her soiled clothes still scattered across the furniture. "Ugh!" she recounted later to a police lieutenant, as she casually inspected the cop's streamlined shoulders. "Talk about creepy!"

Mr and Mrs Packard did not return the coroner's phone calls and were not interested in funeral arrangements.

Marvin Lee's friends set up a fund so that he could be properly buried in the Mockingbird Cemetery a mile from the city limits, a simple marker over the grave. A few of them attended the funeral. The parents did not.

"Didn't he have a wife?"

"Yeah, I think ... I guess they never divorced."

"And a kid, I think."

"Well, the boy drowned. Then there's a girl. Poor kid."

Mrs Packard, defying her husband, concerned herself with her granddaughter's condition and helped Patty with the recovery, both its execution and its cost, taking the girl for drives into the country for fresh air exercises, providing Epsom salts for the baths, inquiring into the March of Dimes, and communicating with the nurses with a bit more authority than Patty could have done. She had never particularly liked Marvin Lee but now she felt sorry for his child and did everything she could to make the rehabilitation easier, so that slowly Eleanor could walk again with only the slightest trace of a limp.

"Learn to walk straight with maybe just a little sway," her grandmother instructed, "and that'll take some of the limp away. That's it, like a sweater girl."

It was about a couple of years after his son's death that Mr Packard fell, literally. He was on a stepladder in his garage repairing a ventilation duct when the ladder suddenly wobbled and overturned, sending Mr Packard falling twelve feet to the cement floor, cracking his skull. His wife tried to sue the manufacturer of the stepladder but upon investigation it was discovered that Mr Packard had placed the ladder on an uneven level, so her suit came to nothing. She settled into a comfortable widowhood; they had been married 36 years.

Evidently the teachers didn't know or didn't care why Eleanor was repeating her seventh grade year. They knew about her mother's unhappy marriage and her father's untimely, unseemly death and they treated Eleanor accordingly. She became the whipping boy for the more advantaged students; if someone was to be reprimanded she was the easy target because she had no authoritative protection. It was about this time that she lost interest in "scholars" and scholastics.

Eleanor's high school days began in an oddly unexpected post-war atmosphere of prejudice and pessimism. Perhaps because of the rumors surrounding her home life and the illness which made her seem pariah-like, she was not popular. Often when she approached a table of girls in the library they would suddenly stop whispering and glance at each other in smiling silence. Boys treated her with an easy admiration which didn't register respect. One day she was seated alone in a nook area of the side campus when she was approached by a boy who was among the school's most popular. She was instinctively flattered.

Casual: "Hi, Eleanor."

"Oh, Hi, Glen."

"How are you?"

"I'm okay. You?"

"I was wondering … what're you doing Friday after school?"

"Well, nothing. Nothing planned."

"Well, I was wondering … would you like to go for a ride?"

"Oh, Glen, that'd be nice."

"Sure, we could go up to the Point. It's pretty up there. A picnic, maybe."

"Oh, sure. That'd be fun."

"Sure. It'd just be about four of us."

"Four?"

"Well, yeah, me and Rooster and Broderick and maybe Jonesy."

"I – uh, you mean with their girls?"

"Hell, no, just the four of us. You'd have us all to yourself."

She stared at him. He was openly grinning at her. "We'll get some beer, you know, have a ball."

She rose from where she was sitting, looked away, then suddenly limped away. "Hey!" he yelled after her.

From then on she had contradictory reputations as a tramp and a tease. She withdrew from all activities and did poorly in her classes, concentrating on courses that might help her take care of herself, such as Driving and Home Economics. Basketball and soft ball, of course, were out of the question.

Her leading lady days were suspended, so that when the Senior Class presented an historical drama she played a background lady-in-waiting, not the queen, portrayed by the principal's daughter. Never mentioned in the school paper, not invited to parties or the prom, she had become an outcast.

It was in her Senior year that Eleanor finally made an impression, but outside the school circles. An art exhibition was held in the school's cafeteria and all students were encouraged to participate. Most of them created Degas imitations or Norman Rockwell imitations, but Eleanor was different. She spent hours in her dark-blue room designing unique mandalas with poster paint, dried flowers and pebbles. The staff thought they were very strange, but Mrs Elaine Fletcher, head of the Fletcher Institute of the Humanities for Young Ladies had been appointed judge and she was impressed, cited the mandalas as the best works in the show, and awarded Eleanor the First Prize. "Well," the principal confided to the librarian, "that Mr Fletcher, he was an atheist. She's probably one too."

The Fletcher Institute of the Humanities for Young Ladies, founded in 1920 by Mr and Mrs Elias Fletcher, was a red-brick ivy-choked building located only three blocks from the high school, surrounded by a wrought-iron fence and entered by a Chasity Belt gate. Eleanor, on leaving high school, was offered a scholarship there for a minimal tuition — "Which I can't afford!" Patty exclaimed.

"Of course not," her mother-in-law replied dryly. "Nobody expected you to. I'll give Eleanor a loan, which she can pay back when she becomes a famous … whatever." In fact, Eleanor's future was uncertain.

Eleanor began in the Institute with three subjects: French, taught by Madame Just, creative writing and dramatic reading, taught by Mrs Fletcher herself, and Art History and Application, taught by Mr Pola, the only man on the staff besides the Master of Music Theory. Mr Pola, thin and dark and with a slight accent, was not at all Eleanor's type, which had developed distinctly into beefy and bourgeois, but he was bright and serious and treated his students with patience. He showed a special interest in Eleanor when she limped into his classroom and gave her obvious attention, approving her abstract art but gently criticizing her representational efforts. He often put his hand on her shoulder while discussing her efforts.

One afternoon Mr Pola asked Eleanor to stay after class and when she had he asked if she wouldn't like to join him at Trina's for refreshment, Trina's being a lacy tea shop a block from the campus. "No, I wasn't born in Italy," he answered Eleanor once they had ordered their black tea and hot cross buns. "I was born in Boston, but I lived in Italy many years, mainly in Rome and Florence, studying. I didn't like Venice, too wet and cold." He placed his hand lightly on Eleanor's. "I'm sorry if I seem a martinet."

Eleanor wasn't sure what a martinet was but answered "Oh, no, Mr Pola, not at all." Gently she removed her hand.

"Can't you call me Milan?" He leaned toward her, smelling of a fine cologne, perhaps English Leather.

"Well, of course. I – I'm sure you were a very good student."

"Oh, I suppose so. I copied mainly, you know, statues, paintings in the Uffizi and so forth. I have dozens of sketches."

Eleanor made the mistake of saying "Oh, I'd love to see them."

"Would you, my dear? I'd like to show them to you. I live in the Hill Apartments, right over here."

"How convenient."

"Yes. Would you like to come up and see a few of my sketches? I think they would help you with your studies."

Eleanor hesitated. "Oh, well, I'd like to see what you've done. You seem so accomplished, so European."

Milan laughed softly. "Yes, Eleanor, please." Then: "Is it difficult for you to walk?"

His apartment was surprisingly un-Bohemian, with second-hand furniture and banal reproductions, a large kitchen, a combination living-dining area, a small bathroom and the bedroom looking out on the street, curtains closed. After he had taken Eleanor's coat he went into the kitchen. "Let's have a glass of wine, shall we?"

Milan put Boccherini on the phonograph, handed Eleanor a glass of Chianti, then settled down beside her with his large portfolio tied with a yellow ribbon. She felt cosmopolitan and soon had a second glass of wine as he discussed Italy.

His sketches began with two Davids, Michelangelo's and Bernini's, the famous Perseus, the Rape of the Sabines, and a pastel rendition of Caravaggio's testa di Medusa. "Now, here, these are originals, some sketches I did myself."

"Oh!"

The first of the originals depicted a bearded youth standing nude and erect, the next a young woman on her knees before the same youth, her hands caressing his thighs, then the two standing together, his head in the woman's shoulder.

"What do you think, Eleanor? There's more."

"They're very artistic."

"I knew you'd appreciate them. You are so much more sensitive than the other girls in the class, so much more receptive. He draped his arm around her shoulder, lifted his wine glass.

"Here's to you, Eleanor, my Botticelli!"

"Botticelli? Oh, no!"

"Oh, yes, dear Eleanor. Here's a toast to your beauty, rising from the sea." After the second glass of wine her head was slightly buzzed and before she had realized it he had unbuttoned her blouse and unclasped the belt to her skirt.

"Oh, I don't know, Milan, perhaps … "

"Not perhaps, my dear. Let's live this moment. Just you and I as though in the Renaissance." Lifting her gently, he led her into the bedroom. Placing her on the bed he cooed: "This will be easy, Eleanor. I have this thing for protection. You have nothing to worry about," as he removed her underclothes. She was just vaguely aware of his warm heaviness and the unpleasant moving about, the animalistic grunting. He never even undressed.

To her relief it was over in no time, and he was bending over the side of the bed. "Oh, yes," he panted, "the ladies like me. Are you hungry? Do you want something to eat?"

On the contrary she felt nauseous and desperately wanted to leave. He didn't try to stop her as she rapidly put on her clothes and his "Thank you, oh thank you, my dear" was ignored. Once outside she limped to the bus stop and sat there in a daze. So that was it, all the romantic hopes and dreams, the giggling fantasies, just absurd groping and grunting. She hadn't even participated, had certainly not enjoyed it. For a moment, just as the bus pulled up she thought she was going to vomit but the urge went away. She wanted to get to the cottage and forget the whole thing. "Cat got your tongue?" Patty asked when Eleanor couldn't eat and didn't speak. No answer.

In the days that followed Mr Pola studiously ignored her, not commenting on her work, not coming near her. He paid more and more attention to Kathryn, another student, and perhaps he invited her to Trina's for tea and pastries. But there was nothing obvious, nothing openly suggestive.

Eleanor couldn't resist. To three of the other girls she asked: "Do you think Mr Pola is flirtatious?'

"Not to me he isn't."

"Wishful thinking, Eleanor?"

"Well, no, I just wondered."

"Ya know, I think he's queer."

Another student: "Oh, no, I don't think so. He's not fat."

In December Mrs Fletcher supervised a reading of "Hamlet", casting herself as Gertrude, older students as Horatio and Polonius, and Madame Just agreed to play the title role, a part which she, like Bernhardt, had once performed in French. As for Ophelia, Mrs Fletcher decided Eleanor was appropriate for the part. The reading was presented on a Sunday afternoon in the Glee Club auditorium, open to the general public free of charge. The elder Mrs Packard brought Patty to the reading, the latter somewhat confused by Shakespeare or Denmark or the combination. She couldn't understand why Ophelia was picking flowers so haphazardly. But afterwards the two ladies invited Eleanor to Valentine's for dinner and told her she had been wonderful.

Mrs Fletcher had also invited an acquaintance of hers to the reading and this was Mitzi Street, a radio personality from station WWYT - We Want Your Trust – where she interviewed people of interest in the studio itself and then took a tape recorder to the streets (the show was called "Street Talk") where she interviewed pedestrians on topics such as the price of eggs or the social inconsideration of adolescents. Mitzi, in her forties, was divorced but had kept her married name for her broadcast persona, calling herself Miss Street.

Like others, Mitzi was impressed with Eleanor's acting and told Mrs Fletcher that the young Ophelia should come to the Little Theater's auditions in January. The amateur company was putting on "The Glass Menagerie" which had been a major success on Broadway seven seasons before. Mitzi had been guaranteed the part of Amanda and she thought Eleanor would be perfectly cast as Laura – but of course she would have to audition.

Eleanor arrived for auditions at the Little Theater at seven on a Wednesday evening. There were only a few applicants on stage to read for the play's four roles, final decisions to be made by the director Mr Snodgrass, seated out front dressed in slacks and plaid shirt. Eleanor felt awkward, though Mitzi Street smiled at her as though they were old friends. Just as Eleanor was seated and introduced, she heard a whispered "Cinderella!" to her right and, looking around, saw a handsome young blond giving her a casual wave. It turned out to be Freddie Mercer, her Prince Charming from third grade. Freddie was attending State on a football scholarship and had come to the auditions with a classmate friend who told Freddie that with his looks he should be in the movies, or at least on the Little Theater's stage. Because she had lost so much school time, Eleanor had fallen a grade behind Freddie and barely recognized him. He recognized her from a newspaper photo from the art competition. She had forgotten her childhood crush on him, and now he didn't interest her at all.

Once the casting had been completed – Mitzi Street as Amanda, Eleanor as Laura, Freddie as the Gentleman Caller, and his friend Bill as Tom – the rehearsals began. The women in Make-up and Props found Freddie irresistible and made obvious advances. As for Eleanor, she found the set designer Harry Buckmaster very attractive and decided she would make her advances to him. Harry, tall and rugged, didn't seem interested in the on-stage aspects of the production, though occasionally he would take a role as a favor to Mr Snodgrass when the director found casting unfavorable, but rather in the technical details.

He had some good ideas, as when the Gentleman Caller first glanced at Laura, and Harry saw to it that an instantaneous vision of blue roses flashed across the back screen. Eleanor would often stand near him, compliment his ideas, and ask for his opinion rather than Mr Snodgrass' ("Well, you should ask Dick about that"). It was the wardrobe mistress who warned Eleanor that though Harry had been divorced for several years he had a steady girlfriend, a dangerous-looking brunette, who was usually backstage. Neither Harry nor the brunette was particularly interested in acting, though Harry had been praised for his Mister Roberts a few seasons back and his friend, to be near Harry, would sometimes take small parts, an onlooker in "Street Scene" for instance. Eleanor learned they lived together and would sometimes go out with the children from his marriage, a daring arrangement for that time and place. Rehearsals went fairly smoothly and Mr Snodgrass approved of Eleanor's portrayal of Laura and, surprisingly, of Freddie's sensitive performance as the Gentleman Caller. Mr Snodgrass and Mitzi would have long huddles discussing her Amanda; they didn't always agree.

Wardrobe provided Eleanor with a single costume, a plain grey muslin gown, to which were added lace collar and cuffs for her long scene with Freddie.

One evening after rehearsal Mitzi invited Eleanor to a coffee shop and when they were settled she casually observed "Harry's a good-looking guy, isn't he?"

"Who? Oh, Harry. Oh, yeah, I guess he is."

"Well, let me tell you: Rachel is very jealous."

"Yeah, one of the girls told me."

"So … so be a little careful, Eleanor. Rachel spoke to Dick about you."

"Oh? I don't know why. No need."

"Okay, just … be careful." Mitzi sipped her coffee. "Oh, Eleanor, I meant to ask you. At Fletcher's did you have a teacher named Pola, Milan Pola?"

Eleanor was afraid she crimsoned. "Mr Pola? Why, yes, he's an art instructor."

"Well, he was. Elaine tells me he's been fired. He tried to seduce one of the students and she told her parents. Quel scandale! He said the girl asked for it, he said a couple of the girls asked for it. Did he … did he ever make a pass at you?"

"Noo, he was a little flirtatious maybe, but," Eleanor felt herself turning red again and was afraid Mitzi noticed it, "he's, you know, very European," she ended weakly.

"Okay. I just wondered. At any rate, he's fired." She forked off a piece of napoleon. "Mm, you know, I'm going to have you on the show Wednesday at noon if you can make it, my 'What's Doing' show. If you can make it."

"Oh, really? Oh, that'd be wonderful."

"Yes, you and Freddie and Bill. We can talk about the play and our roles and all that. Dick likes the idea."

"I've never been on radio before."

"That's okay, I'll prompt all three of you. You have a lovely voice, Eleanor. You'll do fine."

So Eleanor, Freddie and Bill arrived at the WWYT studio Wednesday morning for the noon broadcast. The receptionist, quite taken with Freddie, smiled: "Oh, yes, you're with the play. Miss Street's expecting you. I'll call her."

Mitzi herself came down to the lobby and escorted them to the recording room where the interview would take place. "Now just relax and be yourselves. We're going to talk about the play and I'll ask you about yourselves, your folks and so forth." Slight shaking of Eleanor's forefinger. "Well, I'll be asking the guys some family questions. Eleanor and I will stick to girl stuff. Right, Eleanor?"

At noon a technician stood in the sound booth and fingered off the seconds, then smartly indicated Mitzi. They were on the air with the introduction of a jaunty tune. "Well, Hi, friends, happy noontime, I'm

Mitzi Street bringing you my 'What's Doing' show this sunny Wednesday. 'What's Doing', the show that lets you know what's going on. Today I have three exciting young guests who are all appearing with me in the Little Theater's new production of 'The Glass Menagerie', that wonderful play that was such a smash on Broadway. Now, yours truly is playing – well, let's be honest – I'm playing an old battle ax and Eleanor here is playing my daughter. Eleanor, how's it feel to be the daughter of an old battle ax?"

"Oh, Mitzi, it's such a thrill to be on the Little Theater stage with you. And I want your listeners to know you're the very opposite of an old battle ax. Really, folks, she's so sweet and patient."

Mitzi's eyes hooded for just a second, but then she responded: "Why, thank you, Eleanor, thanks so much. And what about you, Bill? Now, your character Tom gets awfully annoyed with Mama sometimes. What do think of Tom?"

"Well, I agree with Eleanor, Mitzi, you're the greatest. But I'm afraid Amanda – that is, your character – gets a little difficult for a guy like Tom. He's kind of, well, disappointed in life."

"Yes, he's a sensitive young man and I'm sure his mother gets on his nerves. Now we have Freddie who plays the Gentleman who comes to call on my daughter. Now, Freddie, both you and Bill are students at State, is that right?"

"That's right, Mitzi! Go, Grizzlies!"

"And you're on the team, I understand."

"Yes, ma'am!"

"And where are you on the gridiron, Freddie?"

"I'm quarterback."

"I see. And confidentially, ladies, Freddie is very easy on the eyes. Come see for yourself when we put on 'The Glass Menagerie' starting this coming Saturday."

And so the fifteen minute interview continued and concluded, Mitzi's audience learning that Eleanor was a student at Mrs Fletcher's

Institute, that Bill was studying to be an engineer, and as for Freddie – "Well, right now, Mitzi, I'm majoring in football."

That night at rehearsal Mitzi told Eleanor she seemed very easy on the radio, very professional. "Let's keep in touch after the play, Eleanor. We may have use for you at the studio" to which Eleanor answered: "I'd like that."

The production, as it turned out, was a success, with a full house every night at $3.00 a seat. Mrs Packard brought Patty, who didn't like the play at all and wished that Eleanor had not been in it. The local critics were less than demanding, so that all the actors got good reviews, especially Mitzi, but also Eleanor and of course Freddie was compared to a popular movie star. Mr Snodgrass congratulated them all, though with professional coolness, Harry gave Eleanor a distant smile, while his Rachel ignored her completely.

Mitzi was as good as her word: when Eleanor had finished her final year of French and basic philosophy and piano instruction, Mrs Fletcher told her that Mitzi had arranged an interview with the chief at WWYT, and that Eleanor would probably take over the 'Street Talk' show, which Mitzi was giving up in favor of a more serious news programs. ("Good morning, ma'am, I'm Eleanor Packard and this is 'Street Talk'. What's your name?" "Myrtle." "Well, Myrtle, let's talk about this new stadium they're planning. Wow, one million dollars! Tell us what you think of that.")

The spring Eleanor turned 22 she left the cottage and moved into the Cricket on the Hearth Apartments not far from the studio. She rented a one-bedroom flat on the first floor with a small garden off the living room area for $50.00 a month, which she furnished with modern designs, assisted by Mitzi and Mrs Fletcher. Taking out a loan from her new bank account (helped once again by Mitzi), she purchased a Ford for $1,500.00. The garage space in the apartment complex cost another $10.00. Eleanor had become a successful young woman, sporting stylish subdued suits and blouses, wearing her auburn hair in the fashionable gamine style and backing her Ford into a parking lot space where her name was stenciled.

A couple of months after she had moved into the Cricket on the Hearth Apartments there was an unpleasant occurrence. An older woman who lived alone on the same ground floor as Eleanor had one Sunday evening invited a young man, a stranger she had met in a tavern, to her apartment where he spent a couple of hours. The next day, when the lady came home from work she found that the French doors leading into the living room from the garden had been jimmied open, the apartment had been ransacked and many valuables were missing. Though she was mortally ashamed, she had to call the police and file a report. The news spread though the complex like wildfire, and Eleanor was alarmed. When she told two ladies at the studio about it one of them said: "Oh, my dear, you should keep a firearm, just to be safe. That neighbor of yours is lucky the guy wasn't that crazy Englishman."

"I don't know anything about firearms," Eleanor objected.

"We'll ask Jerry to help you. He was in the Marines. He knows all about guns."

Jerry was a stocky Latino with acne scars and an overbite working as a sound assistant at the studio. He escorted Eleanor to Frank's Firearms where he advised her to get something compact, easy to handle. "A Smith & Wesson, that's for you. Here you go, the .38 Special. Let her hold it, Frank. There. Feel okay?"

Eleanor was uncertain.

"I'll give you a few lessons, Miss Packard. You'll get use to it, you'll see. You'll need ammunition."

Eleanor paid $80.00 for the .38, an amount included in her bank loan, and put the weapon in a shoe box on the top shelf of her clothes closet. As he had promised, Jerry gave her lessons in an empty lot and she slowly got use to the aiming and recoil, slowly but surprisingly efficient. Jerry and his father, another ex-Marine, called her Annie Oakley.

In the years that followed, though her radio personality was popular, Eleanor was increasingly alone. She was never invited to a restaurant or a costume picture. Every once in a while she would invite Patty over, but they had nothing to talk about. One evening Eleanor treated herself to dinner at Valentine's. Once she was seated she realized that Harry and Rachel were seated two tables away with his children. They had obviously observed her when she came in but they pretended not to see her, carefully paying attention to each other.

The Little Theater was presenting a romantic comedy and on a whim Eleanor decided to attend the auditions, the first time since she had played Laura. Mr Snodgrass did not acknowledge her when she stepped on the stage and sat down, paying more attention to a pretty teenager testing for the ingenue. When the girl had finished the director called out: "Well, yes! It looks like we've found our Julie!" While Eleanor was reading for the role of the older woman, Mr Snodgrass chatted with a stagehand, then called out: "Okay, that's fine, thanks." The Little Theater was a thing of the past.

It was during this period over the next few years that WWYT made the transition from radio to television. Cameras were installed on sets with diorama backgrounds depicting the city's skyline. Cameramen were hired from New York or specially trained at the studio. Jerry, for instance, attended ad hoc courses at State and apprenticed to a New York professional before becoming a chief cameraman both on the indoor sets and at outdoor locations. As a feature "Street Talk" was no longer an option so Eleanor was brought into the studio where she interviewed executives and kitchen-table inventors on a Friday two PM show called "Getting To Know You". Because of her limp, she was always seated throughout the program, and fortunately she was photogenic. Eventually she was also made anchor of the evening news format, displacing Mitzi and an older man who was retiring. Mitzi herself had become a producer by this time, having no interest in appearing before cameras. The Little Theater stage was one thing, but close ups were out of the question. She was now in her fifties.

One afternoon Eleanor had entered the conference room (or the Green Room as Mitzi theatrically called it), a large high-ceilinged place with low magazine-splattered tables, over-stuffed furniture, a coffee machine and tea table, where Mitzi took her arm. "Oh, Eleanor, I want you to meet someone", then calling across the room "Stieg! Oh, Stieg!" A large reddish-blond brute with bright blue eyes and a vulpine smile came across to them from the coffee table. His shirt and trousers might have been work clothes.

"Steve?"

"No – Stieg. Stieg! I'm a big dumb Swede."

"Oh, Eleanor, don't you believe him. He's a big smart Swede, and he has an adorable little boy. How is Victor?"

"Aw, he's a loose cannon."

"Ah, the terrible twos."

"I guess. He wears May out, and you know she's hard to wear out. We got another one on the way, you know."

"So I heard. Stieg, this is Eleanor Packard, our 'Getting To Know You' hostess. You've seen Eleanor on the air?"

"Sure I have." Stieg grinned somewhat slyly, enclosing Eleanor's hand in his golden-haired paw. He winked at her: "Hey, you're prettier in person."

"Oh, thank you. Your name it – it's Swedish?"

"You bet! Stieg Ekberg."

"Eleanor, you know Ekberg Lumber out on Harris Boulevard."

"Of course. I've passed it many times. So you're the owner."

"Sure am, like my dad before me."

"Oh." She paused, thinking of questions to ask, as she had been trained. "Oh, so it's a family business."

"Sure is, my dad left it to me. But he made me start at the bottom, hauling sawdust."

"Now, Eleanor, you'll have plenty of time to interview. Stieg's our next guest on 'Getting To Know You'." Mitzi smiled and motioned towards the couch. "Why don't you two get acquainted. Eleanor, you can tell Stieg how we run things around here."

"Can I get you coffee, Miss Packard? Cream and sugar?"

"Just a couple of sugars, please. And, please, call me Ellie – I mean Eleanor."

When she returned home that night Eleanor looked in the mirror and thought Eleanor Ekberg; and in bed she dreamed of his bull shoulders, the rugged features, the electric blue eyes. "I'm in love," she whispered in the dark.

The Friday afternoon broadcast went smoothly, Stieg relaxed and friendly. "Today we're talking with Mr Stieg Ekberg, owner and operator of Ekberg Lumber. Welcome, Stieg!" They learned that his father had been born in Sweden, had sailed to America as a twenty-two year old, married a nice Swedish girl he had met at church, and had established his lumber business in 1918, ten years before Stieg was born. Stieg had been married to his wife May for six years. They had a boy Victor, named after Stieg's father. Did Stieg have siblings? Yes, his older sister Pia had moved back to Stockholm many years ago with her husband, who was setting up a practice there.

Now, let's talk lumber. Your customers are … ? Oh, ninety percent contractors. We open early, six AM to accommodate them, and they all have my direct line. And what are the most popular woods with contractors? Pine and cedar, ash and oak. How many people do you employ? Well, it fluctuates but with sawyers, salesmen and secretaries it averages about 200.

The show over, Stieg grinned with relief. "Well, we did it, huh? I tell you what. I don't know about you, but I could do with a drink. Why don't you join me downtown?"

"Oh, I'd love to, Stieg, but I have the five o'clock news."

"Well, that's okay. After the news then. Do you know Brad's?"

"I know where it's at."

"Meet me there, say six-thirty. I'll buy you a drink. We'll be two old show biz pros."

"Okay, I'd be pleased." She was more than pleased, she was extremely excited. He was attracted to her, she could feel it.

Brad's was a sports bar in the warehouse section of the city, hung with pennants and posters, a long oval counter in the center with one television set showing a prize fight and the other a basketball game. Stieg was seated at the bar by himself when Eleanor limped in and he motioned her over with a light wave of his paw. "What'll ya have?" he asked when she had settled herself on the uneven stool and glanced around at the pugilistic patrons. "Oh, just a glass of red wine, please."

"Done!" He called the bartender over. "A glass of red wine for the lady." He himself was drinking a Budweiser.

She suddenly felt awkward. "Uh, you're done for the day? No more lumber?"

"Done for the day! And I don't have to worry about going home, because May's staying at her mother's for a couple of days with the kid." He looked at Eleanor. "So I got all night to prowl."

"Well, that's interesting."

"Yeah. There's a steak house a couple of doors down. Let's have dinner there. What dya say? Unless you got a date."

"Oh no. No, I don't."

"Then let's have steak. My treat."

The steak house was more or less an extension of the sports bar, darker and a bit more sober. Eleanor and Stieg were led to a booth near the back where a matronly type in ruffles took their orders and brought red wine and beer. Stieg leaned back. "I really enjoyed doing the show. It was fun."

"It was nice having you. It's unusual to have such a man on the show. I mean so big and so … "

He was regarding her somewhat sleepily. "So?'

Eleanor laughed nervously. "I mean so brawny and all."

"Does that intimidate you?"

"Oh, no!" She looked at him squarely. "You're very attractive."

"Well, I think you're attractive. Though I must say you're not very brawny."

Another nervous laugh. "No, no I guess not."

"Yeah, I had a feeling about you. Still waters run deep."

The steaks arrived. Stieg tore into his rare porterhouse, wiping the blood off his chin, chugging the meat down with beer. Admiring, Eleanor nibbled at her brochette, wondering what was going to happen next.

Having devoured every bite and pushing the plate away, Stieg leaned back again and asked: "What are we going to do tonight?"

"What would you like to do, Stieg? Go to the movies?"

"No, I'd like to see your place. Why don't you invite me over?"

"I'm afraid I don't have any beer."

"We can get some. You going to invite me over?"

"Oh, well ... yes, I'd like to."

He smiled that foxy smile. "I thought so."

It was eight-thirty when they reached the apartment. Stieg placed the beer in the refrigerator while Eleanor poured herself a glass of wine. She put mood music on the phonograph and invited Stieg to sit beside her on the couch, which he did.

Suddenly he asked: "How'd you hurt your leg?"

"Oh! Oh, it wasn't an injury. I had polio when I was twelve."

"I see. Tough." He reached over and put his hand on her knee. "It hurt?"

"Nooo, not much, but it causes the limp."

"Yeah. Tough." He ran his hand over her thigh. "Feel okay?"

"Yes, it feels fine, Stieg."

Reaching his arm around her, he pulled her closer. He smelled of bargain cologne. "You like me?"

"Oh, yes. Yes!"

He literally picked her up like a swashbuckler and carried her swooning into the bedroom where he dropped her onto the bed and pulled off his shirt, revealing a broad chest matted with golden hair. Eleanor was enthralled. A moment later he had yanked off her blouse and rolled down her skirt. "Take those things off," he muttered, meaning her underclothes. Eleanor did as he said while he unbuckled his belt, pulled down his trousers and his striped shorts. It took a minute to adjust a contraceptive, then "There!" he was on top of her, breathing in short gasps.

"Oh, Stieg! Stieg!"

"Quiet! Oh! Oh!" And he was done. "Whew!" he breathed as he rolled away. "Boy, I need a beer."

"Oh, Stieg, it was wonderful."

"Yeah." He staggered off the bed and into the bathroom. Eleanor heard a flush as she slipped on her robe. Then he was back, adjusting his trousers, pulling on his shirt. "I need a beer," he repeated.

Following him into the kitchen, where he was guzzling a Budweiser, she asked: "Wasn't it wonderful, Stieg?"

"Yeah, it was great. I gotta go."

"I loved it. I love you, Stieg."

He cocked his head like a confused puppy. "Well. Yeah." He was tugging on his windbreaker.

"Wouldn't you like to stay awhile?"

"I gotta go. I call May around ten every night."

"Oh." She attempted to embrace him but he was already at the door. "When will I see you again?"

"I don't know. Later. You know." And he was gone.

Eleanor went to bed alone. "I'm in love," she whispered.

In the days that followed she thought he might call but then it dawned on her he didn't have her phone number. Of course, he could contact her at the studio, but he didn't.

She decided she would make the first move and drove to the lumber company one morning. A guard was at the parking lot and asked for her permit, she couldn't enter without authorization. She parked her car on the street and entered the building itself. Another guard. "I want to see Mr Ekberg." Well, a) Mr Ekberg wasn't in the building that day and b) she wasn't on the appointment list to see <u>anyone.</u> She'd have to call and make an appointment.

When she called the switchboard answered: "Good morning. Ekberg Lumber."

"Mr Ekberg, please."

"I'll give you his secretary."

Secretary: "Good morning. Mr Ekberg's office."

"Mr Ekberg, please."

"Mr Ekberg's not in. He's in the field today. May I take a message?"

"Well, this is Eleanor Packard, WWYT. Mr Ekberg was the guest on my show a couple of weeks ago –"

"Oh, Hi, Miss Packard. Yeah, we all watched the show right here. It was fabulous!"

"Thank you. Yes, I wanted to ask Mr Ekberg a few questions about the show, so I thought … "

"Well, I could leave him a message. He could contact you at the studio."

"Yes, but I wondered … Mr Ekberg said he had a direct line."

Silence. "Well, yes. But, Miss Packard, that line is for contractors. Let me take a message."

There were three more phone calls similar to that one and the responses were beginning to sound increasingly tense with dubiety, especially when Eleanor asked for Mr Ekberg's home telephone number.

Eleanor took to driving to the company and sitting in her car across from the parking lot, but she never saw him: he must have had a private entrance.

A long letter was sent but was never answered. A second longer letter marked Personal! in red was returned unopened to her and officially stamped Addressee Unknown.

An appointment was accepted, then refused ("I'm sorry, Miss Packard, there was a mix-up.") Another confrontation with the front entrance guard ended with Eleanor raising her voice: "But he wants to see me! He _needs_ to see me!" She was escorted back to her car.

One Friday morning Eleanor received a phone call while in the conference room. It was Stieg, telling her that he had to talk to her, preferably in an impersonal place. She agreed, having time between her interview show with a modiste and the evening broadcast, so she met him at a coffee shop on the edge of town. When she got there his pickup was in the parking lot; he had already arrived, had ordered two coffees and brought them to a table near the window. He looked grim.

"Now, Eleanor, am I going to have to contact the police?"

"The police? For what?"

"Look. I'm awfully busy lately. I've got a big project with the Jamison company, and I'm having to give May a lot of support. So … "

"So what?" An edge in her voice.

He glanced at her. "So I can't have you following me, harassing me, sending me those nutty letters."

"Nutty? Harassing? Stieg, I'm telling you how much you mean to me."

"Well, don't! You've got to stop."

"But what about the future?"

"That's what I'm trying to tell you. Are you listening? That was one night. Now I won't be seeing you again."

"No, no, that can't be."

Impatient: "Well, it is. You have to grow up. You have to understand."

"I understand. What about my birthday?"

"Your _what_?"

"My birthday. You haven't said what we're going to do."

"Eleanor, it's <u>your</u> birthday. You do whatever you want."

"But with you, Dear. You have to be with me."

"No, I don't have to be with you. Hey, you're becoming a burden, a real nuisance. Let me be."

"A burden? But you love me, Stieg."

"Love you?" He shook his head. "Hey, I don't particularly <u>like</u> you. You've got to stop this. I don't want to see you ever again. Ever. That's it."

"No! You have to be with me. I mean it, Stieg."

"No, <u>I</u> mean it! Now listen, you can't be this stupid: I will call the police. I'm never going to see you again. Ever!"

A long pause, then: "I'll make sure May knows."

He gave her a sharp cold stare. "No, I'll make sure she knows. I'll make sure she knows what a malicious little leech you are."

"Leech?"

"Leech! Witch! Gimping around trying to get what other people have. Why don't you leave people alone?" Abruptly he stood up, seeming to think for a few seconds, then he reached into his pants pocket, pulled out some crumpled bills and threw them on the table. "Here, you've earned this." And, without glancing at her again, he walked out.

Through the plate-glass window she saw him hop into his truck and drive away. She knew she should weep or scream but she couldn't. A couple of customers, half amused, were watching her. She had to get away, she had to get home. After several minutes, she stood up and left the shop, left the dollars littered across the table. She had to get home.

It wasn't until she was back in her apartment at the Cricket on the Hearth that she realized she was cold and trembling, from anger or fear she wasn't certain. Then she remembered she had to be back at the studio for the news hour at five. I should denounce him on the air, she thought, reveal him for what he is, make him pay. Then she had an idea.

Slipping off the floral smock she had worn to the coffee shop, she reached in the clothes closet and pulled out a simple black sheath dress, decided on no jewels, and brushed her hair quickly away from her face. Then she reached into the closet again, brought down the shoe box, and removed the .38. "I'll show him. I'll make him pay." She chose a black patent leather purse and slipped the weapon inside, smiling.

Driving to the studio (thinking: Will Mama be watching? She usually does), Eleanor parked the car in her space. She brightly greeted the techs who were waiting for her: the broadcast was ten minutes away. The makeup man added blush, the stylist brushed back her hair at the nape, and the wardrobe girl checked her dress for lint ("What, no pearls?"), before she limped quickly towards the set, giving Jerry the okay sign. Just as she seated herself behind the desk, tucking her purse in her lap, she heard the portentous staccato of the news hour's theme and a baritone voice calling out: "And now from the WWYT News Room – the Evening News, presented to you by our own Eleanor Packard!"

"Good evening, ladies and gentlemen, and welcome to the Evening News. We've all sorts of news tonight, good news, bad news, but first of all some personal news. Yes, I've got something personal to share with you all. This'll be fun, you'll see." Reaching into her purse she brought out the .38, and when it came into camera range cries and shouts of alarm could be heard from the surrounding staff. Eleanor, smiling directly at the unseen audience, jammed the pistol's muzzle beneath her left jaw and said "Watch me."

This Sad Time

L ATE ONE JANUARY MORNING ADAM LORD FORGOT HIS shoes. He showered, shaved and dressed as carefully as always and didn't realize his error until he stepped on the kitchen's cold linoleum floor. "Gilles," he said, looking down at his stocking feet, "I forgot to put on my shoes."

Raspy-voiced Rochester: "Land sakes, Boss, you gonna catch your death. You puts your shoes on and I'll make a big pot of hot coffee."

"Yes, yes." Adam looked over at the slight grayish-blond man staring at him from the stove. "Yes, I'll go back up. Oh, and, Gilles, maybe a waffle."

Sitting on the edge of his unmade bed, Adam worried "How could I have done that? What would Martha have said?"

Martha had been dead for seven years. They had been married in 1967 when Adam was twenty and she was nineteen. The couple had known each other from childhood, when Martha's father had employed Lord and Dout in a property dispute.

Adam's grandfather Colin had been born in the 19th Century and in the year 1914 (a century before this story begins) the Great War had begun in Europe and three years later he had sailed to France in order to save that noble, bluebloodied country from Hundom. It was there in an estaminet trench (Bonne guerre, dough-heads, spirits and coffee al fresco!) that Colin met the cynical Claude Dout. Strangely, they had been raised only a few blocks from each other and had both as boys displayed an affinity for jurisprudence but had never met till now, here on the edge of Death. The deadly atmosphere must have been a lively stimulant because the two became the best of comrades, despite their disparate personalities, and when they returned to the home of the brave they earned their degrees in the same school and eventually became partners: Lord & Dout, Colin getting precedence because of his two-month seniority. Their personal lives also coincided when Colin fell in love with Linda and Claude fell in love with Linda's best friend Virginia. The two virgins wished a double wedding, snow-white gowns, white blossoms glowing in the pure light pouring through Protestant windows. Within two years Virginia had given birth to Claude Jr and then his sister Joan. And Linda? She mothered the golden-haired Jeff. The child survived, the mother didn't. She died and the boy grew up motherless.

Motherless but a bright boy, Jeff grew up strong, interrupting his apprenticeship with Lord & Dout (alongside Claude Jr) when he enlisted the day after Pearl Harbor and, returning from France nearly three years later (after he, slurping a sorbet framboise, had watched DeGaulle's triumph on the Champs-Élysées), married Joan Dout, his friend's sister, in 1946 and continued law school. (Claude Jr, afflicted with asthma, had been deferred and completed his education while Jeff fought.) All through the war Joan Dout had communicated with Jeff via long magnolia-scented letters on pink floral stationery, telling him about her business expertise: as a teenager she was already a budding entrepreneuse, and it had nothing to do with secretarial school. For her eighth birthday an aunt had presented Joan with a Young Lady's Jewelry Shoppe, being a cardboard box containing plastic ornaments, glass pieces of varied colors, false pearls, and strings of cloth and wire. Joan was fascinated with the prospects and was soon adroit at creating brace-lets and necklaces for friends and relatives. Greatly admired, she was encouraged to progress to more refined glass and semi-precious stones. By the end of the war she had opened a boutique in her mother's potting shed, Joan's Jewelry. Unfortunately, a bijoutier on Main Street (who sold <u>real</u> pearls) objected to even this minor competition and complained that Joan was operating without a license, which was true. She was ordered to desist. Her mother was frightened; her father disdainfully shook his head. But after she had married, Jeff assured her: "Don't worry, Honey, we'll get you a shop, a real shop downtown. You'll see, I'll be your lawyer." And two years later he was.

Joan had not really been a threat to the unhappy bijoutier because she never aspired to genuine jewelry. Her specialty was imitation and after so many years she was so proficient that even the most demanding matrons had difficulty telling the difference. (One of Joan's patrons from the South Martin shop told her that when the lady had worn a varied stone peacock brooch to a concert she was told: "Oh, my dear, aren't you brave to wear that in public!") By this time she had advanced to pewter, fine crystals, agate and jasper.

Jeff and Joan Lord had been married a little over a year when they gave birth to Adam. He grew up healthy and happy, admiring Roy Rogers and excelling in baseball. "He'll make a great lawyer," Jeff decided, "like grandfather, like father" and planned the boy's education from day one to prepare Adam for law school and the bar. Fortunately, the child and the adolescent were both eager to follow his father's trade and enjoyed arguing legendary cases with Jeff on winter evenings, Joan at her drawing board, designing perhaps an extensive collier.

Incidentally, the original founders of Lord and Dout had both died in 1950, when Adam was four, Jeff's father of a heart attack, Claude Jr's of self asphyxiation, Jeff and Claude Jr taking over the business. The two kept busy taking, unlike the famous lawyer of fiction, not one case at a time, but handling on the average six at a time, none of them as melodramatic as a one-eyed witness. Both Joan and her brother dealt with the elder Dout's dexterity handling a plastic bag with somewhat chilly equanimity. He had never been a great presence in their lives, nor in their late mother's.

Adam was in his thirteenth year when three milestones were reached: he began preliminary clerking in Lord and Dout, he met Martha Johnson in the school's journalistic club, and his father first suggested to Joan that she expand her shop not only to a second location (which was done) but begin designs for a plant to be constructed outside the city limits. He had just the site in mind and it could be purchased for a song (okay, an aria) if negotiations were handled wisely. Joan was uncertain at first (her employees in the shops numbered twelve – a plant would mean dozens) but Jeff kept at her with blue prints and budgets until she finally agreed that she would sign the deeds of ownership. She did not want the name of her shops to be the name of the business, and Jeff agreed it should have a separate title. He suggested something classy – Royal, but Joan said No, it sounded like a soft drink. Okay, he said, not a soft drink, good hardcore liquor – Regal! So Regal it became, with an Old English ℜ coronated appearing on the plant's tower and on the company's stationery. Over the next three years the plant evolved into what had been envisioned on the blue prints and Adam visited the construction site constantly, often taking Martha with him, the two of them wearing hard hats, talking with the workers.

Martha Johnson was a bright blonde girl from a middle-class family (her father was a CPA) who read the classics and took rudimentary lessons on the piano. Understanding the legal arguments that Adam presented to her, she sometimes challenged them, calling herself Portia. She enjoyed her visits to the incipient Regal complex with Adam, not to mention the dinners afterwards, were they hamburgers at the Good an' Hungry on Main Street or frog legs at Chez Foch on South Martin Street. (With of course non-alcoholic libations.) Their courtship had begun as shy observation, then equally shy conversations (which theme would be proper for this class?), then movies and dancing. They were made for each other, and Joan loved Martha, wanted to take her into the business. (It turned out that, after her marriage to Adam, Martha managed both shops, the one downtown and the one at Deepvale Shopping Center).

In the summer of 1967 Regal Simulated Jewelry had its official opening. It meant a flurry of celebrations amid the hirings of artisans, mechanics, accountants. By this time it had been decided to forestall the inauguration of Dout, Lord & Sons and allow Adam to test the waters of commerce: in fact, his mother wanted Adam to be the firm's Chief Executive Officer, using his legal experience to protect and expand her investment. Joan Dout Lord, as she called herself, loved to tour the plant dressed in dark gray and <u>real</u> pearls purchased from her girlhood plaintiff, being introduced to the employees and taken to lunch by her son. It was during this same summer that Adam and Martha were married in an opulent Protestant ceremony, banks of red roses, the bride a pink and white princess, red satin dresses for the bridesmaids, tuxedoes for all the men, reception in the city's largest hotel. The couple spent two weeks in Paris and Provence, accompanied by an unobtrusive guide/translator.

When Adam and Martha returned from their honeymoon they moved into a large house in the suburbs, a Dout property as a matter of fact. Within a year they had given birth to a girl named after the company but universally called Reggie, raised in luxury, given dozens of dresses, dozens of dolls, given whatever she demanded by relatives, servants, admirers. She was a remarkably beautiful child, lush dark hair, light blue eyes, exquisite features. People adored her.

It was at Reggie's lavish third birthday party when Joan was caught outside the miniature circus tent (in the still smaller tent, away from the clowns, where adult refreshments were offered) by one of her best customers, she of the peacock brooch, to "beg a special favor". It seems the affluent lady had a cousin-in-law, her husband's cousin, and the poor relative was having difficulty adjusting to life. He was three years younger than Adam and he had already flunked out of two schools, failed at two business ventures, and drifted from job to job. Like Adam, he had married his high school sweetheart, but due to the boy's instability the union was not working out, though the wife was expecting a child. Urban was a sincere Catholic so divorce was out of the question. His wife Susan, a plain girl with modest hopes, had been born (again?) Baptist but converted when she married Urban, learning (with difficulty) the catechism and the names of all the saints on the calendar and agreeing that marital vows were sacred. She came from an insecure family with a fireside secret. But though the marriage was uneven the church would make it firm, she was certain, and the coming infant would add ballast.

And that is how Urban and Susan Pleasance entered the gates of Regal, he as a loud storage area superintendent, (many of his co-workers complained) his wife as a quiet guest at company dinners. Susan was elated with the birth of their son, whom they named Peter, but the blessed event did not balance their marriage. The problem with their marriage was Urban with his unstable temperament and his roving eye or wandering eye or at any rate an eye impatient with connubial responsibility. Not even a year after Peter's birth his father began on weekends frequenting the Good an' Hungry downtown, his favorite waitress being a peroxided flirt named Louella, who served Urban his eggs and sausage with an extra egg and a wink. According to rumor Louella had been married and divorced twice and may have been a mother at some point but that was uncertain. Louella herself was a sphinx with no questions asked. Urban, bright Christian that he was (he held lunchtime prayer meetings), prayed for strength, but one day at noon when Louella intimated to him that she'd like to meet him around three when she got off work he eagerly agreed.

That is how this louche relationship began and lingered for several months. Hot afternoons in a furnished air-conditioned studio apartment. Urban would tell Susan he had something to attend to and it was none of her business and would disappear for a couple of days. This even happened during the week: he would show up for work but not go home in the evenings. Susan was frantic, dealing with motherhood and a missing husband. Like all unhappy wives she had long telephone conversations with her formidable mother who lived in a distant state. Divorce? No, it couldn't be. Help? Well, the Jefferson estate was considerable, and Susan could always depend on her mother for financial support, though Mrs Jefferson's Protestant prejudices increasingly disapproved of Urban and his Catholic ways. (Susan's mother was a widow, her husband having died in middle age under mysterious circumstances.) With her mother's help and the needs of her child Susan thought she could endure the marriage. But the worst had yet to come.

One afternoon Louella told Urban she was going to have a child. <u>What</u>?

"Yeah, I found out last week. But it's okay, I can take care of it."

"Oh, Lou, I'm so sorry. We should have been more careful."

"We. Yeah."

"Well, I'll make sure you get the best of care, the best doctors."

"Huh? Oh, Urbie, I know this sawbones, he's reliable, he'll take care of it. For a price."

"What do you mean?"

"I mean get rid of the kid. This guy can do it."

"What do you mean? Get rid … you can't mean … oh, Lou, only the Lord can take a life."

"Oh, Urbie, grow up! I've been here before. It's quick and easy."

"Oh, no. No! Only the good Lord can take a life! We'll do it … well, my way. The child must be born."

Louella's conclusion: "Jesus!"

Urban went to confession and it was the priest who suggested something that had not occurred to the errant father.

"My son, you can adopt this child."

"But, Father, it was born in sin."

"We are all born in sin, my son. By giving this child a clean honest home you can eradicate all the sin committed." The priest paused, then added: "Of course, your wife must be told. You must confess everything to her."

The thought of confronting Susan with this story left Urban frozen with trepidation, but he steeled himself and one evening, in the kitchen of all places while she boiled carrots, Peter watching gravely from a high chair, he told her everything about the coffee shop, about Louella, and the unfortunate result.

Susan turned off the sauce pan, sat down at the kitchen table staring at Peter and asked: "How long?"

"Oh, not till spring."

"We'll need another room."

"I'll see to that. We can build an extension. Your mother can help us."

"Yes, she will."

"Oh, Susan, you're being so good about all this. Please join me in prayer."

"No thanks. You go ahead if you want to."

Urban knelt by the kitchen table in prayer. Susan went back to her carrots, sprinkling basil. Never again did she enter his church; never again did she call him by name. (It was "Uh, here.")

So the following May, much against her wishes, Louella, cajoled and bribed, entered an out-of-town hospital and gave birth to Urban's second son. (Father: Unknown) Urban named the child after one of his favorite patriarchs, the chaste Joseph. Adoption papers were processed and signed right there in the administrative offices. Susan was present, complaisant but cold. Louella, who cared nothing about the birth and who received some compensation from Mrs Jefferson's bank, was never heard from again, even in the Good an' Hungry. As for Urban, he cared even less and wanted to forget the date of Joe's nativity. It was Susan who saw to it that she end Louella never met and that the staff at Regal was told that Urban and Susan had generously adopted a poor abandoned boy. There were sidelong glances and whispers, but the story was accepted.

A month after little Joseph's misguided arrival, Martha Lord entered the city's most prestigious hospital to be delivered of a second daughter, this one named Delia. Adam was extremely proud, handed out phallic cigars, and glowingly assured Reggie she had a sister, an event they had tried somewhat dully to prepare her for. Reggie was not thrilled. Up to this point the world had revolved around her but now at age five she discovered she had to share this world with another girl. Reggie watched from aloft as the newcomer received cooing and presents, gratifications that were rightfully hers. She began developing her adult personality.

The four children Reggie and Delia, Peter and Joseph grew up separate from but aware of each other, frequently meeting at company parties and picnics. Slowly they became acquainted.

Joe was always estranged from those presumed his relatives, apart from the arrangement, not a part of it. His mother rarely spoke directly to him, rarely made eye contact. His father was distant with forced fatherly attention, and his brother Peter actually said one night, perhaps instinctively, "You're not one of us". So it came as no great shock when his father set Joe down at the age of six, like a priest at confession, and explained to him that he had been adopted – not the whole story, of course, no Louella, no muggy studio apartment, just that Urban and his wife had discovered this wonderful boy and had adopted him. But then the wonderful boy asked a piercing question: "Why?"

W-why? Because they loved him so much. The child continued evenly: "When was I born?" The year was given, he was six years old.

"What date? When is my birthday?"

"Well, uh, well, the nuns at" {the convent? The clinic? The charcuterie?} "at well, no one was really certain. And that's why we've had your birthday with Peter's."

Yes, Joe had always wondered about that. Joe's birthdays had always been a void or avoided. On a certain date in December there would traditionally be a party where Peter got a cake, Peter got presents, Peter got compliments, and Joe got a card illustrated with an adorable puppy saying via speech balloon "Hi, Fella! I want to be your friend!"

He slowly became convinced that Peter was right, he wasn't one of them. It was the same with school, where teachers talked down to him or ignored him as skillfully as his mother. It was in the fourth grade when he finally heard the word that was to define him, snarled by an older boy in the mens room. "Didn't you <u>know</u> that, Dummy? That's what orphans are!"

"I was adopted."

"That don't mean a damn thing, Dummy. You ain't got no real mother or father."

But it was only in his teens that he began hearing the other rumors, the ones that said his father ran around, that he was going with some waitress for a while and she was Joe's <u>real</u> mother, not that old scarecrow at home.

From that day on Joe's emotions were frozen. He loathed his father, his mother, and Peter. He began mocking them openly and (the only thing he had in common with Susan) mocking the church that meant so much to Urban. In late adolescence he would grin during dinnertime blessing and then regale anyone and everyone with his version of the Creation: "Well, you see, the Old Spook had nothing to do one week so he says to himself 'I think I'll create Heaven and Earth'. A can-do guy, this one, a go-getter, he's ambitious! So he rolls up his sleeves and gets to work: rocks and trees and clouds and rainbows. But that wasn't enough. Oh, no, then he starts on the <u>real</u> stuff, cats and dogs and finally Man! Oh, Man! Then he realized Man's got nothing to do – he's <u>there</u>, but he's got nothing to do! So the Old Spook builds factories so Man can work himself to death and whore houses so Man won't get bored and orphanages to house the little brats till <u>they're</u> old enough to go to the factories, the almighty meat grinders. And the Old Spook looked at the whole thing and he says to himself: 'Yeah, that's good. That's hotdamn good!' He was proud of himself and treated himself to oysters and steak. And beer, the old alky."

Vengeance is mine.

By the time he was twenty Joe had grown six feet, with a blonde crewcut and light sardonic eyes. Women looked twice.

Women also looked twice, thrice at Peter, though he didn't possess Joe's somewhat Satanic intensity. He had never liked Joe and was different from him, but not extremely different. Like Joe, he resented living in a rented house on the "other side" of town while the Lords lived in a mansion or near-mansion in the Hylands district. Like Joe, Peter was aware that their parents did not like each other and that their father was barely tolerated in the Regal plant, coming close to dismissal a couple of times. Urban's uneasy temper and his constant Bible thumping were equally grating, many of the women on assembly objecting to his easy-going familiarity during his explanations of Exodus. "And Moses, he married this girl named Zipporah, which means something like bird. Scholars think she was black, a big-breasted black girl you know like Sadie in the lunch room." Urban concentrated on the Old Testament, one of his favorite stories being of Samson throwing himself away on that good-for-nothing good-looking tramp. Urban became obsessed with mean good-looking tramps.

The fates of Peter and Joe were diverse. Peter went to the university west of the city, studying business administration, toiling nights at a Dairy Queen, creating cones and sundaes. He met his mistress at the Dairy Queen and he treated her as well as he could. Joe used his acerbic charm to get a job in the mail room of the local <u>Morning Bugle</u> in the center of the city, worked his way up to copy room and eventually became a cub reporter on accidents and other disasters. He and the <u>Morning Bugle</u> had a flair for disaster. He was a classic cub, with red suspenders, sleeves rolled up to the elbows, cigarette jammed beneath a dark blonde moustache, mulling over coffee and local crime. Unlike his brother, Joe enjoyed a series of girlfriends that he used and discarded.

Delia, the youngest of the two Lord sisters, first noticed Joe when they were both ten years old during a Regal picnic celebration at a mad tea-party game, complete with over-sized cups and magic tea pots from which popped surprises. Already at ten Delia was a romantically receptive girl, excited by the look of a boy's rough and tumble and the fragrance of his Lucky Tiger hair tonic. So it was with Joe, unusually aggressive and handsome for his age, unafraid indeed contemptuous of adults, demanding of his peers. Delia, a sweet and subdued daughter, was naively impressed. Seven years later she was still impressed, though she had barely spoken to Joe, barely dared to speak to him. She confided in no one, there was no one for her to confide in, least of all her older sister. Reggie was not the confiding type.

Reggie had grown into a beautiful young woman, dark brown hair which she wore to her shoulders, sloe sky blue eyes. Slim and shapely, her movements like those of a cautious doe, she loved smart clothes, real jewels, and flattery. She sheltered a strong aversion to humanity but conversely, oddly, had an almost immoral greed for any admiration or desire she might sense from others. Deeply aware of her own attraction, she loathed ugliness in any form, having contempt for age or deformity. She mocked any man who did not fall under her spell and instinctively disliked other girls, even, especially her sister, whom she considered coy and hypocritical. A sneer always underplayed Reggie's smile. She was distrusted, even by those under her spell, considering men as things to be exploited. They fell into her trap despite their inmost warnings.

Then in Delia's nineteenth summer something odd and unprepared-for happened. She was browsing in Duval's, deciding on a cocktail dress for a brunch being given in Reggie's honor when she heard a surprised "Why, Delia!" behind her and turning saw a worn middle-aged woman staring at her, repeating "Why, Delia, you look lovely! I thought you were your sister!" It was Mrs Pleasance, dressed in a plain coat and an outmoded straw hat, whose somewhat unpopular husband worked in the Regal plant. After some strained chit-chat the older woman suddenly, unexpectedly said: "You know, both my sons are home this weekend and I'm making a meatloaf, Peter's favorite. Why don't you join us, Dear? We'd love to have you." After some hesitation (the dark gray and the black were both stunning) Delia answered she'd be glad to. So Saturday evening found Delia à pois in the Pleasance living room listening to Urban explain a passage in Judges while Peter watched the silent (though evidently hilarious) television, Joe flipping through an old National Geographic. Delia was the only young lady there, the girlfriends either unknown or uninvited.

Before the soup was served the company had to sit through Urban's repetitious blessing, Susan and Peter staring at the table, Joe finishing off the fascinations of Valparaiso. As they settled into Susan's meatloaf (served with apple cider) the chef observed to no one in particular:

"Hasn't Delia grown into a pretty woman?"

"Yeah," Peter answered without thinking, "at first I thought she was her sister." Joe just stared across the table at Delia, gave her a sly wink. As they were having after-dinner coffee in the parlor, listening to a recorded choir singing psalms, Joe, smelling of that childhood Lucky Tiger hair tonic blended with a bargain counter cologne, sat behind Delia and whispered "Feel sorry for me?"

"Mm?"

"Dealing with these idiots."

"Oh … "

"You deserved a lot better than this." He ran his index finger up and then tickled her back. Her heart raced. Delia was either frightened or infatuated.

She was infatuated. Though of a gentle nature Delia had the passionate temperament of a Russian heroine, enough to realize that she was in love, and like Tanya or Natasha she knew, riding home that night on the city bus, that she was going to make a bold move. A week after the Pleasance dinner Delia took another bus downtown and entered the offices of the <u>Morning Bugle,</u> where she was pointed in the direction of the cub's desk, way off in a corner behind two other larger desks.

Sitting down, she waited for Joe to come back from the water cooler, then smiled and said "Good morning!"

"Well, Miss Lord, good morning. To what do I owe this pleasure?" Joe jerked behind his desk and lit a cigarette.

"Oh, just a social call to thank you for the lovely evening. I sent your mother a note."

"Oh? Well, maybe she can read it, if you stuck to two syllables. You really <u>enjoyed</u> that mess? Lady, you are – oh, well."

"Yes, I did." Pause. "I – I thought I'd invite you to lunch." She glanced at him hesitantly.

He stared back. "Well, sure. I'd like that. We can talk."

Twenty till noon Joe escorted Delia a block away to the Deadline, a newspaper bar-restaurant that was getting crowded but was still comfortable, Joe finding a booth near the front.

The waiter greeted him by name and brought him a Budweiser. The lady? "Just a glass of red wine, please." IDs were not mandatory. Unlike the <u>Morning Bugle,</u> the Deadline, protected by City Hall, was liberal. They ordered cheeseburgers.

"So you liked Pop's Bible-thumping?"

"He seems devout."

"Devout? He's cuckoo."

"He's … very nice. And your brother too."

"Oh, yeah, Peter the Great. Out to conquer the world. The business world."

"He seems sincere."

"Oh yeah. By the way, where did you meet Mom the other day?"

"At Duval's. The dress shop. I was looking for a cocktail dress for Reggie's party. We're giving her a party. She's getting married, you know."

"Mom at Duval's! Ha! No, I didn't know about your sister. Who's the lucky guy?"

"A very nice man. He works at the plant … "

He worked at the plant and he was considered a very nice man. When the chief accountant Mr Somebody retired Adam had realized there was no one in the department with the venerable experience of the outgoing employee, so he placed ads in the two local papers for an experienced accountant, extensive references, excellent salary. The position was taken by Morris C Stephenson who, due to some labyrinthine childhood anecdote, was always called Mack.

Husky and healthy, he was of an affluent family, his father a bank vice-president, an uncle having run for a state office. Adam was impressed, though Mack's opiniated nature was a bit forward for Regal's conformity. Even as a kid Mack had had a mind of his own. When his buddies had dreamed of traveling the world's tropical jungles to "meet interesting people and kill them" Mack had admired the men who marched in protest and burned their cards, though he also felt sorry for the thousands who adventured into the jungles and never returned. Later in college, though a football jock, Mack made fun of stadium adoration and pressroom hysteria. Mack was the type of stalwart who was popular with both men and women, and he had been working at Regal for several months when he was invited to a dinner in the Conference Room at Bill's Steak House located on the same highway as the Regal Simulated Jewelry plant and this is where he saw Reggie, twenty years old in red satin and rubies. Mack was thirty, a well-fed specimen, swelling out his chest and squaring his jaw, something that caught Reggie's interest and her instinct for conquest.

Asking around, Mack discovered that Reggie was the oldest of Adam's two daughters, the younger being Delia, pretty but no Reggie. Mack was an old-school gentleman, so he approached Adam and asked if he might come to call. Adam in turn spoke to Reggie whose chief concern, before the swelling chest and squared jaw, was: "Does he have money?" Assured that the Stephenson family was more than solvent, Reggie agreed to be approached, dated and then seriously courted. Several months later Adam announced the engagement of Miss Regal Lord to Mr Morris C ("Mack") Stephenson, the wedding to be announced in the near future. Delia was to be the maid of honor so she and her mother planned a June afternoon party to be held in the back yard rose garden in honor of Reggie's happiness. Then sobriety intervened: Jeff Lord died of a heart attack at home, age 72 , just (as a matter of fact) when Delia and Joe were having cheeseburgers at the Deadline. Like his father Colin, Jeff died unexpectedly, leaving Adam and Martha in shock and at a loss how to comfort the ageing Joan Dout Lord. Joan went in mourning for the rest of her life, a period of two years, and the black cocktail dress that Delia was going to wear to the rose garden she wore to her grandfather's funeral with a long black shawl. Reggie, escorted by Mack, wore a purple dress and an impassive demeanor.

Reggie's wedding, postponed till December 7th, a Saturday, was (like her birthdays) a lavish affair, Reggie in white lace, Delia and the bridesmaids in lustrous pink, flowered by rose buds, the chapel decorated by pink and red roses. Delia invited Joe, which meant his family, sharing a pew, Urban in rumpled blue corduroy, Susan in green checks and a little green cap, looking for all the world like an elf. Joan was still in mourning so she wore black and Martha, in deference to her mother-in-law, wore a gown of subdued mauve.

Like her parents twenty-three years before Reggie and Mack held their reception in a downtown hotel and then spent two weeks in France. When they had returned they moved into a purchased and furnished home in the Hylands district of the city, provided by Mack's parents and Joan Dout Lord. All seemed serene. But while Mack was still a bachelor, he had bragged to his confreres that once married he was going to sire the son of all sons and he made it clear that was his principal motivation in taking a wife. Unfortunately, it was in a suite at the Ritz that he learned his dreams of parenthood were <u>not</u> shared by his bride. She would satisfy all his male inclinations, yes, but she had absolutely no intention of becoming a mother: the idea of physical burden and blown-up deformity were abhorrent to her. "But, Lamb," he would argue, Lamb being an obligatory conjugal term picked up from his father, "we have to have a child. What will people think?"

"Think? They can think what they like. But I am not having a child."

"But, Lamb … " By the time Mack and the lamb moved into their new home, he was a disillusioned husband. And remained childless.

Ten months later, about a year after his father's death, Adam decided to return to the firm of Lord and Dout at the request of Claude Jr who had never married and who had been working with a silent partner. It turned out the partner had been making too many not-so-silent stipulations, so Claude Jr had decided to end the relationship and begged his former partner's son to re-enter the profession, with his expertise in contracts. Adam agreed, passed the bar exam a second time, and became the older Claude Jr's junior partner, with an office overlooking Main Street South. And who was to take Adam's place at the plant? Who else but his admired son-in-law Mack. Reggie's husband displayed all the brawny bonhomie of a successful business man, but he was becoming increasingly unhappy with his cold marriage and his wife's prolonged luncheons, which were beginning to last beyond two, then beyond three hours. "How was lunch Tuesday?" he would casually ask Delia, and she would reply: "Oh, Joe didn't show up. An extra or something." "Oh, you weren't having lunch with Reggie?" he'd pursue, and Delia would follow with "Oh, Reggie would never have lunch with me. She was probably with one of her pals." Delia suspected nothing but Mack was becoming uneasy.

Ironically, Reggie had first become aware of Joe through Delia's chattering. He was so smart, so manly, so sure to become a star reporter with bylines and a big salary. "Why don't you invite him over for drinks and dinner some night?" Reggie suggested, and Delia, Innocence itself, did. It was a night Mack happened not to be home. That very evening Reggie had made it clear to Joe, though glances and gestures, that she was ready to experiment beyond marriage and

Joe himself had responded to these hints with his own subtle but ruthless attention.

At the same time Mack took over as Regal CEO, a year after his marriage, his wife and Joe began meeting in a small discreet hotel downtown. Reggie rented the room on a regular basis, telling the desk staff that it was to be her "headquarters" while she shopped and dined. Joe would take a taxi over from the <u>Morning Bugle</u> and the two of them would spend two hours in the room, then go out for a late lunch nearby, at the risk of being seen by acquaintances. Then Reggie would return to shopping and Joe would return to sensationalistic journalism, worlds, incidentally, they respectively loved.

One afternoon, wading into chili, Joe laughed: "Big sister!"

"Oh, God, don't compare me to her."

"Oh, there's no comparison, trust me."

Reggie glanced across her egg salad. "What does that mean?"

Joe grinned. "What'd ya think?"

"Well, still waters run deep. I wasn't sure she knew the difference."

"Oh, she knows the difference. I promised her a lollipop."

"Well, just don't take her seriously."

"Hell no!"

"She's a real little leech and not to be trusted. And a liar. She used to tell Dad all sorts of stories about me when we were kids."

"Were they true?"

Reggie smiled. "Well, sometimes. But she's a squealer and a liar, not to mention stupid. Don't trust her."

And almost a fortnight later, as though answering a summons from the angel of Doom, Delia slipped smiling into a booth in the Deadline and whispered: "Oh, Joe, I'm so happy. Guess what? I'm going to have a child."

Joe paused half-sip. "You're going to do <u>what</u>?"

"I'm going to have our child. I found out yesterday."

"<u>Our</u> child? Your child, maybe. Leave me out of it."

"B-but, Joe, it's your child. We can be married now." Poor Delia.

Joe almost spit out his beer. "Oh, no, Sweetheart, <u>you</u> can be married now – to any sucker you can find. But me, I'm not the marryin' kind. This baby can be a bastard like his pop."

"But, Joe, we have to get married. It's your child."

"Says who?"

"Well, the law. Joe … "

"So sue me. Better yet, get rid of the kid. It's easy. Oh, and by the way, I <u>don't</u> like children."

"Get rid … ? You mean … ? Oh, no, I couldn't. I want this baby."

"Great. Then have it. Just leave me out. In fact, just stay away from me from now on. You're a nuisance. And you're probably lying!" With that he stepped out of the booth and called out: "Hey, Karl, forget the burger. I gotta go."

"Sure, Joe. And the lady?"

"Who knows? Who cares?" And he was out the door.

Delia scrambled out of the booth and followed him, but he was too fast, trailing a waft of cigarette smoke. She was left alone. Weeping on the sidewalk, watching him disappear around a corner, she knew he was out of her life forever and there was nothing she could do about it.

Laying siege to the <u>Morning Bugle</u> or paying lachrymose visits to the Pleasance home were out of the question. Legalities? She couldn't go through with anything that humiliating. She could only turn to Adam and Martha. They suspected who the father was, a young man they did not trust any more than they admired his father, but were quick enough not to press Delia into confession. They only told her they would support any decision she made. "I'm going to have the baby," she said. And she did. In the months that followed Reggie's old room was transformed into a nursery and Delia actually took courses on how to be an efficient and affectionate mother.

One afternoon in early March Martha visited Reggie at her home and Reggie, reflected in a mirror brushing her hair, said: "So little sister's going to be a mother. And who's the proud papa?"

Martha sank into a chair by the vanity table, staring at her elder child. "It's not important. He's a scoundrel."

"Mm."

"The important thing is we stand by Delia, we help her in every way. Is that clear, Reggie?'

Reggie stared back at her mother's reflection. "Well, of course, Mama, of course."

One afternoon in early April Mack left his office on the sixth floor of Regal Simulated Jewelry and took the elevator down to the third in order to visit the Purdue man who had replaced him as head of Accounting when he himself had been appointed chief. The prodigy was out, however, so Mack decided to have coffee and a sandwich in the third floor lunchroom. Taking his tray to a terrace overlooking the parking lot, he found a small table in the corner, concealed by a large plant, where he could pursue <u>Fortune</u> in private. After a few minutes two secretaries giggled onto the terrace, taking a table far from his but close enough so that he could overhear their gossip. It was a revelation.

"I've heard they meet in some crummy hotel downtown about this time of day and <u>she</u> pays for it."

"Well, natch. Have you seen him?"

"I'm not certain. Does he work here?"

"No, he doesn't. His father's that creepy old guy in Shipping, the one who holds prayer meetings."

"Oh, God, no! That Pleasant or something?"

"Pleasance. The guy's name is Joe and he's Hollywood Heaven."

"Oh! Tall, kinda blond with … those eyes!"

"That's him, Girl. So you're wondering why Mrs Stephenson is footing the bill?"

"Oh, yeah, now I remember. I've seen him here with that dopey old father of his. But wait a minute – I've seen him with her kid sister too, the quiet one."

"He gets around. But Mrs Stephenson is the one who's got the hooks in him. Even though … and this is strictly confidential."

"Oh, sure."

"I hear the younger one is preggers."

"No! Who by?"

"Who do you think? But like I said, big sister's got the money he's after. I don't think he's the marrying kind."

"What time is it?"

"We got a couple of minutes. You know, I wonder if Mr Stephenson knows."

"Poor guy. He's so nice. And kinda cute."

"Oh, well, you know what they say. A fool's paradise. We gotta go. That new guy, Powell, he's got the eye of an eagle."

Mack sat frozen, the sandwich uneaten, the magazine unread, stunned. Traffic sped on the highway far beneath him.

He had his coat and his keys with him so he didn't return to the sixth floor. He went to the parking lot, then drove to Pelham Park, where he sat a full hour on a bench in front of the replication of a fountain in Rome.

She never loved him. Did she love another, that – that illegitimate son of the holy man in the basement? Did she love anyone, even her parents? It finally dawned on him he had never heard her say a sympathetic word. Where others would have said "Oh, that's awful!" Reggie would say "Ugh, that's disgusting!" She had a cold nature devoid of sympathy. He decided, sitting there, watching the splashing fontana, that he would confront her, find out exactly what she would say when he accused her.

He got home late. "You're late," she said. She was wearing slacks and a halter, both deep pink. "Do you want your scotch?"

"Yeah, I could use a drink." He waited till she had handed him the old fashion glass before he began: "I heard some gossip today."

"Oh? You listen to gossip now?"

"Well, I was cornered, a captive audience, sort of."

"Anybody I know?"

"Yes, as a matter of fact. A couple of secretaries were talking about an affair going on with the son of one of the employees and … and a married woman."

She turned to face him, martini in hand. "Oh? Which employee?"

"That spooky old character in Shipping, Pleasance."

"Yeah, I've heard he spouts the Bible a lot. I barely know who he is."

"But you know his son, his illegitimate son. His name is Joe."

"What are you saying?"

"You know what I'm saying. I thought there was something up. What you're doing, Lamb, is called infidelity."

"Oh, yeah? And what about you?"

"What do you mean?"

"All those cute little quote unquote secretaries?"

"Nothing!"

"What about sweet Georgia Brown in Accounting?"

"All this hasn't got a thing to do with reality. This is just your vile imagination at work."

"What if I start investigating?"

"Investigate all you want to. They'll find everything there is to find about you and that two-bit Wild Bill Hickok. I can divorce you and when I do you won't get a dime from me, Lamb, not a dime."

"Who needs you? I'm worth a fortune."

"Reggie, you're not worth two cents. I'm sorry I ever married you."

"<u>You're</u> sorry? Do you think I've enjoyed this? Get a divorce, who cares?"

Of all days it was the day after this confrontation that Adam in his legal office got a phone call from Mack: Joan Dout Lord had been hospitalized. She had been attending a meeting in the Regal executive suite when, on rising from her chair, she had suddenly toppled over, her hand striking the table when she instinctively reached out, her head striking the carpeted floor. They rushed to her aid to find her conscious but disoriented. An ambulance was called, she was taken to the emergency room where the family physician diagnosed a transient ischemic attack and ordered her admitted to the hospital.

That night Mack moved into the Olympic Club, then to a modest hotel. The divorce proceedings began in May and by the end of June Mack no longer had a wife.

Adam and Martha were dismayed by the separation and they were shocked when, two months after the divorce, Joe moved into the Hylands mansion with Reggie and the two began living in sin in every sense of the word, hosting loud parties featuring champagne and prescription drugs with the occasional **ménage à trois.** Ironically, the same autumn Peter Pleasance married his long-time friend, affectionately known as Darlene the Dairy Queen (a reference to their first meeting), and they moved to the capital where he became the manager of a large agricultural supply company and she worked as a substitute school teacher. Over the years they had three children, two boys and a girl. He was estranged from his parents.

Mack had been living in the Brockton Hotel for two months when Adam suggested his erstwhile son-in-law live with him, Martha, and the budding Delia. Mack had his own room on the top floor and always dined with the family. When Delia gave birth to a boy in October she gave Mack the right to provide the name. "Michael," he decided. He had always liked the name Michael.

Joan Dout Lord had never approved of Delia's decision and she saw the child only once, when they brought it to her bedside in the hospital. The matriarch's second TIA, transient perhaps but stronger than the first one, had made her increasingly acerbic and now, a vase of red carnations by her bedside, an unread Edna Ferber by her pillow, she peered querulously at the infant through her bifocals, never attempting to hold or even touch it, and observed: "An unattractive child."

"Oh, Grandma!" Delia exclaimed.

"Ah, Ma," Adam laughed, "you know all babies are ugly."

"Not _that_ ugly," Joan said.

"Oh, Grandma!" Delia was beginning to choke up.

But Joan was right. Little Michael had a puffy, ungainly appearance inappropriate to infancy and it only got worse as he progressed into childhood, with a droopy face that never laughed, never cried, a progress that surprised everyone except the absent Louella.

Joan Dout Lord never saw that childhood. A third stroke ended her life at 73, carnations faded and So Big unfinished, a little more than two years after her husband's death. The Regal plant closed in mourning for a full day and a momentous funeral was held, all the employees invited. Reggie was told she could attend the funeral alone but she declined. She had never liked her grandmother's superiority, perhaps because it interfered with her own.

Mack, never a man of conventional expectations and with a special rapport with the underdog, formed a paternal attachment to the unfortunate Michael. It was he who absorbed the doctors' advice and their glum predictions, revelations which Mack told Delia in grave secrecy. He became the family's Gibraltar, escorting Adam, Martha and Delia to Chez Foch, under new management, for coq au vin, to a touring company's presentation of a Broadway comedy, or to a classy afternoon concert of chamber quartets in a Methodist church (the pastor complaining privately of secular music being played in a holy precinct). It was Mack who arranged the engagement of a private nurse, she looking after Michael from seven AM till (sometimes) late in the evening. Michael, who at two was still not talking, was becoming an increasing problem. The family depended on Mack more and more and eventually, of course, the evenings out for boeuf bourguignon and light entertainment were strictly between the Gibraltar and Delia.

He went to the plant every morning, to his office on the sixth floor, and it was here he met Mrs Stark, a widow d'un certain âge, auburn and raw-boned, wearing a tweed suit and carrying, in place of a purse, an attaché case. She kept their appointment promptly at nine and, after a couple of pleasantries regarding the products of Regal, she told Mack the reason for her visit. She was a supervisor at Dix Institute which was located outside the city behind stone walls and a formidable gate, and it was her duty to place "guests" after it had been deemed possible for them to enter the outside world. Dix was not an asylum but rather a "home" for the abandoned, the uncertain, those not ready or able to deal with the pragmatic demands of everyday life. There was one "boy" there who had been a "guest" since the age of eight and was now twenty years beyond that point in his life and was employing space at the institute which might be better filled by a younger visitor. She wanted to place him at Regal because he had displayed a gift for creativity, in both design and colors: Mrs Stark was convinced he could be a valued employee in one of the departments at a manufacturer of simulated jewelry and, she added frankly, his salary was freely negotiable. Dix would find him lodgings near the plant and he was perfectly able to take care of himself. With continued frankness she confessed that his personality was a bit … well, odd, and that some simpler intellects might be confused by his satirical humor. Mack was intrigued and agreed that Mrs Stark could bring the boy by for an interview the following Monday, meeting in the CEO office with the personnel supervisor.

And so Gilles came to Regal. Born under suspicious circumstances, he had been dropped on the front steps of the Dix Philanthropic Building (separate from the institute) when he was three days old. A stunted, sickly child he was tended by the medical staff at Dix until it was determined he was healthy enough to join the other "guests" in the communal living quarters and eventually the class rooms. Five foot five and frail, he was not proficient in sports and so spent very little time in the playgrounds. He did spend a great deal of time in the recreation room, entranced by the images of the television screen and becoming obsessed by the films of the thirties and forties, both the classics and the Bs, memorizing their plots and dialogues.

At Regal he was first given a position in receiving, his responsibility to check and re-check all deliveries, making sure they tallied with the orders. He was alert and efficient enough, but his strange humor confirmed Mrs Stark's caveat. When told that a delivery had to be managed immediately Gilles would answer in raspy respect: "Land sakes, Boss, well, of course, I does what you says, Boss!" Or in a Southern falsetto: "Oh, fiddle-dee-dee, don't you ever think of anything important?" Needless to say, many of his co-workers were confused by the responses and therefore made angry. Urban Pleasance had to interact with him and confirmed to others that Gilles was a monster, a celestial mistake.

Gilles' only confidant at Regal (discussing the immorality of world systems at lunchtime) became Ralph, a custodian and, because of his vaguely Marxist views, something of a misfit like Gilles. Ralph lived in Coontown outside the city limits where he kept a token farm left to him by an uncle. Beyond the house itself was a stable where Ralph kept his beloved horse. He was capitalistically proud of the horse because it made him a man of property, a man of importance, a chevalier, a caballero. One evening Ralph was in a nearby tavern when a boy ran in yelling that Ralph's place was on fire. Jumping into his truck, Ralph raced frantically to his little farm: it was the stable, engulfed. Twenty or so people were standing around watching. (Had a fire brigade been summoned? Perhaps, but it never arrived.) Ralph, screaming and sobbing, had to be dragged back from the flames. The horse was roasted alive. No one thought for a glancing moment that is was an accident, but that is what it was judged. About a week later Ralph put a shot gun in his mouth and fired, leaving his wife and child in despair. After that Gilles ate his lunch alone.

A limerick was found on a wall near the loading dock:
There once was a man who was black
Who had a fine horse, not a hack
But those who were able
Burned down the man's stable

So the man and his horse won't come back

No one knew where the limerick came from; it was painted over.

Later Gilles was transferred to Design where he created a lapis lazuli lizard pin with tiny red stones for eyes. Complimented by a spinster supervisor, he alarmed and confused her with a Provençal-accented response: "Ah, ma belle, come wit me to zee Casbah." She was not amused, and the imitations were becoming increasingly unappreciated.

Mack and Delia were married during the Christmas season almost exactly four years from the date he had married her sister. It was a simple ceremony held in Adam's living room, which had been tastefully decorated by Martha, Mack dressed in a three-piece dark blue Hart, Schaffner and Marx, Delia in a deep rose shift with a diamond necklace to match her ring. Claude Jr attended with a man at least a generation his junior who, he said, was training for the law. Michael was there, google-eyeing the decorations, being sharply warned "No! Michael, no!" when he attempted to bat the balls off the tree, and being served his roast duck with cherry sauce at a separate table near the fireplace. Needless to say, Reggie was not invited.

The couple spent their honeymoon in Manhattan, staying at the St Regis, going to see "Madama Butterfly" at the Met, shopping on 5th Avenue. When they returned they bought a home in the Perth section of the city, near the hospital where Michael had his tests and treatments.

Time streamed on, the three couples – Adam and Martha in the Hylands, Joe and Reggie three blocks away, Mack and Delia across town – rarely communicating beyond notes or an occasional phone call. Holidays were awkward. The time came when Time became tremendous, reaching a new century, in fact a new millennium, a frightening prospect, and nearly two years later erupted that disastrous morning supposedly foreseen in the 16th Century though Our Lady mis-prophesized both the month and the year. The shock of this event led the <u>Morning Bugle</u> to reach sensational extremes, its front page inspired by Joe himself: BASTARDS!

It was six years after *le grand* Roy *d'effrayeur* had made his appearance that Martha died unexpectedly, diagnosed in June and succumbing in October. She was buried in the plot reserved for her and Adam beyond a spray of dogwood trees on a hillside far from the other plots. Adam, Delia, Mack and Claude Jr were gathered at the gravesite when Delia suddenly gasped "Oh! Oh!" A taxi had driven up and parked beyond the dogwoods and Reggie, dressed in a pink-striped dress with a full skirt, had stepped from the back seat and, peering through dark glasses, stood uncertainly for a moment near a tree. "Oh, God!" Delia cried. "You! You — " Mack restrained the second Mrs Stephenson and Reggie quickly ducked back into the cab and it sped away. The sisters never spoke again.

It was after Gilles had mocked a supervisor ("Aw, ya mug!") that Mack was told there was a decision among the employees: Gilles simply could not stay, regardless of how efficient he was. The most outspoken of the employees was Urban Pleasance, who was convinced that Gilles was the spawn of the Devil, that he was going to doom them all to Perdition. "Oh, Jesus," he prayed aloud at the lunch table, "save us from this unholy corruption!"

Mack turned to Adam for help, Dix having informed the younger man that once a "guest" was released from the institute he was not accepted back. Adam had been alone in the Hylands for two years since Martha's death, except for a cleaning team that came in once a week, and so Mack's solution was to have Adam "adopt" Gilles as his valet, his factotum, a position which Gilles took to with that peculiar humor completely compatible with Adam's frame of mind. Gilles took Delia's old room as his and had all his meals at Adam's table. The factotum himself became the sous chef (Adam's chef having semi-retired from Chez Foch) and supervised the cleaning of the house and the control of the finances, at which he was unusually proficient. This employment went on for several years.

One evening Mack and Delia (leaving Michael with a special nurse) had been invited to Adam's for caneton aux navets and during dinner

Mack revealed a bit of news from the Regal plant: Gilles' old nemesis Urban Pleasance had been complaining more and more about the lighting conditions in the work place. It was consistently too obscure for him, too dark for him to do his work. But it wasn't just at work he complained, it was in his rented house also. "Don't you pay the electric bills?" he barked at Susan. Finally in the months after the duckling dinner, even Urban had to admit it wasn't the electricity at fault, it was his eyes. He was persuaded to visit an optometrist and was given the diagnosis: macular degeneration. It degenerated from dimness to darkness, and he was becoming blind.

His employment at Regal was terminated, he was given a pension, but his stay at home was difficult. Susan complained she couldn't take care of him alone, they couldn't afford a nurse, and she turned to Joe for help. Joe's response was that Urban and Susan should give up the house, sell the furniture, and move in with Joe and his friend, the generous and kind-hearted Reggie. Susan saw at once that was an unlikely arrangement; she belatedly but determinedly went home to Mother in a distant state, leaving Joe to reap the rewards of his father's pension, disability, and his auctioned property. The blind man's presence in the Hylands home didn't interfere with its messy dinners and its midnight parties. In fact, Urban was usually the center of entertainment, the guests re-arranging the furniture just for fun.

Joe had brought over several cardboard boxes of Urban's belongings and one contained stacks of magazines, but underneath old back copies of <u>Catholic Digest</u> he came across several publications of a decidedly different character.

"Oh, boy! Oh, Pop, you old poop! Hey, look, everybody! Get a gander!"

All the others gathered around and a shrill female shriek of laughter was heard. "Oh, no! <u>Ladies of Leather</u>! Oh, no!"

"This one's wearing black chiffon – well, almost."

"Look at the colored girl – with a whip, yet."

"Those heels! How do they <u>walk</u> in those things?"

"They don't walk, Baby, they <u>stomp</u>!"

Urban called out weakly: "Joe, all that is personal."

"Personal? I'll say it is, ya dirty old coot."

"Oh, no, look at this one! 'Beg for it, bad boy'. Oh, no!"

Joe looked over at his father, seated in darkness. "That's it! No dinner for you tonight, bad boy!"

"Hey, make him beg for it." Howls of laughter.

And so life continued for Urban with his son and Reggie, year after year, and each Christmas Joe entertained their crowd with his version of the Nativity: "There was this babe, see, like a teenager, named Mary and she married this old barf-bag named Joseph. Yeah, Joe – that tells you he's a loser right there. So Joe, he's old as dirt like Pop, and he likes 'em underaged <u>but</u> he can't cut the mustard. So Mary comes to him one day and tells him she's preggers and Joe says <u>Huh?</u> You <u>know</u> I can't cut the mustard and she says Never you mind, she got a visit from a really weird guy who told her she was going to have a baby boy and Mary says Whoa, fella, not with old No-noodle I'm not and the weird guy says Aw, forget that loser, the kid's father is going to be – hold onto your seats, folks – Almighty God! Yep, God himself is going to come take a look-see at Mary, do the hot stuff and bingo! she's going to give birth to the Son of God! Now, everybody, I mean <u>everybody </u>knows that this tramp's been laid by every shepherd in a fifty-mile radius, but they all go along with it for poor Joe's sake and they call the kid Beloved or Bojangles or something and that's why we're all celebrating here to-night getting drunk as horny skunks. End of story. Like it, Pop?"

"Very amusing, Joe. And very typical."

"Shut up and finish your egg nog. It's your bedtime."

Following Claude Jr's death Adam retired from the law; the practice, according to Claude Jr's will and Adam's approval, was handed over to the senior partner's protégé and the protégé's wife, the name was changed to Smith & Beecham, and the emphasis evolved from business contracts to pre-nuptial agreements and divorce proceedings.

After his retirement Adam spent most of his time at home being looked after by Gilles. He noticed that his memory was beginning to falter, that he couldn't remember things that had been told him only a few minutes before. Then on a January morning he sat, fully dressed, on the edge of his unmade bed trying to remember why he had come back upstairs. Then it dawned on him: his shoes, he hadn't put on his shoes. He couldn't go to the office without his shoes. But wait a minute, he wasn't going to the office, hadn't been to the office in years. What would Martha say?

One day he was worrying over a crossword puzzle when suddenly he looked up and realized he had no idea where he was. He told himself not to panic and, looking around, he eventually recognized a small table, a plant, a picture and slowly (just how slowly he was never certain) the separate objects all came together and he knew he was in his living room. Rising uncertainly, he entered the kitchen where Gilles was cleaning up. "Gilles," he asked, "am I losing my mind?"

The factotum dropped into a kitchen chair, "rolled" the arms, swiped his hand across his mouth and growled: "Why, ya young whippersnapper, ya only lose your mind when ya die! Didn't they teach you <u>anything</u> in that school ya went to?"

"Oh, well, you're the genius at Blair. I wasn't sure."

But it got worse, Adam wandering around in the rose garden nude, Adam attempting to eat a bar of soap. In desperation Gilles traveled by bus across town to Perth, asking advice or help from Mack and Delia, but all they could offer was financial support and private nurses. The idea of placing Adam in "someplace" was out of the question. They wanted to have nothing to do with Reggie and her paramour, and of course they were dealing with the latter's son Michael who at the age of twenty was a heavy responsibility with his physical events, his narcolepsy, and his startling tantrums. So Gilles returned to Hylands and protected Adam as well as he could. But it got worse.

When Reggie learned of the problems three blocks from where she and Joe lived, she decided this was the perfect time to "extend" her property. By this time she had dieted and sun-bathed herself into a russet desiccated stringbean, eternal admiration gone; and Joe, due to an excessive consumption of beer, had lost his matinée idol appeal. The two of them, all smiles, cookies and good wishes came for a visit and promised Adam all their assistance. "Why?" he asked.

"Because we <u>love</u> you, Daddy! Oh, please let us help you." And so the two entered the house, turning it into Nightclub East. The first thing they did was discharge the nurses ("<u>We</u> can handle my father!") and then the Chez Foch chef ("Sortez, idiot!"), then Reggie decided the Snail didn't need a bedroom — he could stay in the basement's mother-in-law, Daddy too for that matter. So both Adam and Gilles moved into the dark area downstairs with a bedroom, a guest room, a bathroom, a kitchenette and a doorway opening onto the stone steps leading up to the rose garden. The house's main floor was transformed into a ball room, the French doors removed so that guests could dance easily from the living room area to a buffet table set up in the banquet hall.

Their first grand party was held in June and coincidentally on that month's Friday the 13th. The party's theme was Bad Luck, the décor included cracked mirrors and black cats, and (appropriately and literally) it was a dark and stormy night. Guests entered screaming and shaking their umbrellas. Joe was getting drunk on beer, the others on gin or whiskey. Skunky smoke drifted through the rooms. For entertainment Joe had brought his father and now set him up at the buffet, feeding him a ham sandwich and forcing drinks on him. Then came time for tricks and games and Urban was led out to the center of the room for Blind Man's Bluff. Obstacles were encouraged, to the shrill enjoyment of the guests. Thunder rumbled outside and rain splattered against the windows.

Adam and Gilles were watching from the kitchen, Adam, gray and vague, visibly disturbed. A child's voice, plaintive with precise enunciation: "Mr Minnelli, should I cry now?"

"We can all cry now. It's the crying time." Looking down, he added: "Gilles, it's time to go."

Adam took Gilles by the shoulder and led him slowly down the stairs to the basement, pulling two suitcases out from under the bed. "It's time to go," he repeated. "I can see what's coming." Laughter and loud music boomed through the ceiling.

Gilles, in his own voice: "Yes, I know. But there's a storm."

"We have to go. Anything's better than what's headed our way. It's time to go."

"Yes, I know. We have to go."

It was a decision they could not refute. Slowly they packed the two bags, folded five hundred dollars in a plastic kit, and opened the door to the outside world. Making their way up the stone steps, Adam held the umbrella while Gilles carried the bags. Then, without looking back, they disappeared into the darkness of the storm.